THE CITY OF SILVER

MOONSONG, BOOK I

By
David V. Stewart

CONTENTS

For Houkje

WESTERN
DEIDERON
IN THE SIXTH DOMINION

The City of Silver

Prelude: Power

"Tell me, Vindrel, what is power?"

Sarthius Catannel turned his head away from the rail for a moment to regard Claire as she stepped across the threshold to the small balcony overlooking the courtyard. Below his shock of blonde hair, his green eyes stared at her with the same vacant stillness as when she had met the man years before. She felt a chill and drew her robes around her body tightly.

"Power, sir?" Vindrel, the dark-headed captain of the guard for as long as Claire could remember, stood beside Sarthius, his uniform of blue and green crisp as always.

"Yes, power." Sarthius stared out of the balcony as Claire crept up to stand close behind him. "What does it mean to have power? To be powerful? This philosophical quandary has been on my mind of late." She could smell the fire in the courtyard below, and quickly pieced together what was taking place. She didn't want to look, but knew somehow, she would. In the end, she would not be able to avoid it. Sarthius would see to that.

"Power..." Vindrel looked down for a moment. "Power is the ability to exact your will. To do what you wish."

Claire noticed the flintlock pistol that Vindrel openly carried in defiance of Church Law. It was a generally accepted fact that Vindrel was a *Somniatel,* though nobody ever dared to accuse him. Watching him look out to the courtyard with his familiar stone-cutting gaze, she believed he could, in truth, be a member of one of the strange rustic clans that as much as worshipped the magical and technological heresies of the Dream God, living like savages in wilds of the world. If it was true, it explained much of his retention with the young count; Dream-cultists were valuable sell-swords, just as much for their uncanny, even supernatural, skills as for their lack of ethics.

"Power to do as you wish... A good answer," Sarthius said, "but not quite right, I think. A woodcutter chops down a tree because he wishes it. Is he powerful?"

"He is to the tree," Vindrel said, scratching his thick, black beard.

Sarthius cracked a smile. "So he is. What do you say, Claire?"

Claire felt a lump in her throat as the count's empty eyes met hers again. "I think the woodcutter is not the powerful one in this scenario."

"And why?" Sarthius said.

"Because he can't chop down the tree. He needs an axe. It is the axe that has true power," Claire said, doing her best to stand up straight and look the part of her position as high cleric.

"Spoken like someone who truly understands the Canon," Sarthius said. "I'd expect nothing less than an acknowledgement of the gifts of the Gods of Knowledge to man."

"But it is the woodcutter who swings the axe," Vindrel said. "The axe is just a tool."

"Like you?" Claire said. The words came out with the wrong tone – far too assertive. A bead of sweat broke out on her brow.

"Aren't we all?" Vindrel said, a slight smile parting his beard and bringing out lines around his eyes. "It is Count Catannel that is the wielder, even if the tools can think." Vindrel's eyes were narrowed in the bright light from the cloudless sky, drawing in shades of yellow to his iris.

"I like this analogy," Sarthius said. "But it is incomplete." His lips twisted into the semblance of a smile, though the shape was somehow perverted. He gestured for Claire to approach the rail. She swallowed, feeling the lump in her throat return. She stepped up beside the count, looking out over the ornate stone rail to the courtyard below. There was a raging fire beneath a raised earthen platform, a stage that usually served up executions in the form of hangings. That day, however, the deathly theater would not display such a casual disbursement of criminals. Fire was for apostates of the most dangerous sort. "The woodcutter has as much in common with the axe as the axe does the tree."

"How so?" Vindrel said.

"The axe has no will. No real will, and like you said, power is the ability to exact your will, though it is also more than that," Sarthius said. "The axe is merely doing what it was designed to do." He nodded and smiled at Claire. "By the god Ferral, of course."

"Of course," Claire said.

"Not at all like myself and Vindrel." Sarthius chuckled. "For the woodcutter is also doing what he was designed to do. He too is a tool, serving masters he does not even recognize as such. He cuts the trees because they have value to others, not himself. The trees are merely a means to some other end – his family and livelihood, perhaps."

"That seems like life in general," Vindrel said. "The baker bakes to feed others, not himself. If you don't mind me saying so, aren't we all just serving some other's end with our actions? Even a king may serve the gods."

"I don't mind you saying what you wish. Better than groveling," Sarthius said. "Everyone serves somebody else, thus sayeth wise Denarthal, yes?" He cast a glance to Claire, then turned as another set of footsteps entered.

It was Donovan Dunneal, a man who had been given his naval commission from his high birth and advanced it through a type of brutality that even the court cleric could not avoid hearing about. Claire envied him less that Vindrel, if only because she knew that in the shifting landscape of power on the Isle of Veraland, a birthright was more likely to be a liability than a blessing. At least beyond the Cataling court she had no claim to power, and thus nobody beyond plotting to usurp her.

"Yes, you are correct, my lord," Claire said, choosing to lock eyes with the clean-shaven Dunneal as he approached rather than look out to the courtyard. She said formally, "Our place among all others is the gift of Denarthal. His knowledge is the foundation of our society. Our interdependence and interconnections are bound by his gift of the coin." Feeling awkward staring at Dunneal, she looked down on the courtyard. Only a few people stood to witness what was going to happen. For what Claire expected to see, usually only the most perverse residents of the city enjoyed bearing witness.

"The truly powerful do not submit to such notions of interdependence, cleric," Vindrel said. "The powerful do what they will."

"Exactly," Sarthius said. "I knew I made a good decision keeping you on. The axe would only be truly powerful if it cut the woodcutter, rather than the tree."

"I don't follow, lord," Claire said.

"To be powerful, you must be able to make the wills of others conform to your own." Sarthius gave her a smirk, but his eyes were as calm and still as ever. "To be powerful is to make the system into what *you* want it to be."

"Such ideas are dangerous," Claire said. "In the wrong company, of course. The same goes for your gun, Vindrel."

"Are you the wrong company?" Sarthius said, raising his eyebrows.

"No, my lord," Claire said. "As cleric to your grace and the church of the city, I am merely giving advice for your dealings with the world. You have done much to further the church and its ministry, but there are men who prefer to judge according to outward displays, and not actions."

"I am lucky to have such a wise counselor," Sarthius said. "Action... perhaps that is the last element of power. If you have the power to do something and never do it, who is to say you had the power at all? Yes, power only exists if you use it."

"Otherwise a beggar could claim to be the greatest sorcerer in the world," Dunneal said.

Sarthius chuckled, in a deep and scratchy tone. "Yes, of course. Let us observe an element of power. And of action, for the glory of the church and her holy gifts." He nodded toward the platform below.

The scattered crowd of mostly men began to hoot as the door to the dungeon was opened and the guards appeared, chains between them holding a young woman, her white flesh shining brightly under the noon sun. She was naked, and even from the heights of the small room, streaks of grey grit could be seen on her flesh.

Ardala, Claire thought as she watched the frightened face dart to the men of the crowd. It was only a few weeks prior when she had seen the same woman in the halls of the castle, busying herself with bed changes and cleaning. She was one of the few servants that didn't seem totally worn down by the atmosphere of the place. Eventually, all of them shared the same vacant eyes as the count. Claire wondered silently if her own eyes looked like that.

"So rare to see a mage burned in these all too dry times, eh?" Sarthius said.

"I thought she talked," Claire said.

"She did," Sarthius said. "She told us everything, and with not much effort, I must say. The torturer was disappointed."

"Most disappointed," Dunneal said, casting a sickly look to Claire.

"Yes, but she was lying," Vindrel said. "The Lady was not in the tavern when we went."

"She was telling the truth," Sarthius said. "I could see it in her eyes."

"Then why are you killing her?" Claire felt sick as she watched the young woman being led up the steps. The fire blazed off the end of the platform.

"Because I am a man of actions, not words," Sarthius said. "Whether she lied or not, the result was the same."

"But do you have to?" Claire said. She squeezed back tears as a leather bag was placed around the young woman's neck.

"I do," Sarthius said. "Power does not exist unless you use it. This must be done. For her. For these men here. For all who would betray me. And for the men below, their wives, their children... all the people of Cataling, who must believe not only that magic exists, but that their lord and their church are greater than it."

Claire turned away, covering her mouth. "You... Have no betrayers here, lord," she said through a choke.

"Do you not wish to watch?" Sarthius said. "It is so rare that we see a mage cleansed from the world. I do this as much for the church as for my court."

"No, I don't want to watch, lord," Claire said.

"Then why did you come up here?" Sarthius's eyes remained fixed on the scene outside.

"I just..." Claire took a breath and looked out the door. "Wanted to inform you of the death of King Grasslund."

"That *is* good news," Sarthius said with a smile, still never taking his eyes away from the scene below.

"Yes," Claire said. "It seems that his grief over the excommunication and banishment of his last son was too much for him, and he succumbed to his sickness."

"The writ of ascension?" Sarthius said.

"It is being cleared by the high priest as we speak," Claire said. "We can organize the coronation as soon as the writ has been acknowledged by all the other high lords."

"Good," Sarthius said. "It seems your job will require a bit of haste, Vindrel. I want the Lady here for the coronation. I want the Grand Cleric to see her here with me."

"I have a good idea where she's heading," Vindrel said, clearing his throat. "I'll need a ship."

"I'll give you more than that. Captain Dunneal? Or is it admiral now?" Sarthius smiled at Dunneal.

"I think it's a fitting time for that promotion," Vindrel said.

Dunneal bowed with a smile. "Thank you. I shall not disappoint you, your highness."

"I like the sound of that. Your highness," Sarthius said.

Dunneal smiled. "Your highness, something occurs to me. Need the Lady be present for the coronation?"

"The church *will* observe the law," Claire cut in. She looked down as Sarthius narrowed his eyes at her. "I'm merely letting you know the temper of the Grand Cleric, your highness."

"What I mean," Dunneal said, "is… How shall I put this? What if tragedy were to strike your beloved, and you were to remarry?"

"That would be quite a delay," Vindrel said.

Dunneal chuckled. "We can write whatever story we choose. Right, Claire?"

"Yes, your highness," Claire said.

Sarthius leaned over and looked down at the crowd. His eyes narrowed. "Yes. Who is to say that my wife did not already die, perhaps a month past, and that we held the news for our grief?" He scratched his jaw. "I have considered this. But then I would lose my ties to the Hviterland and the rest of the Northmarch." Sarthius laughed. "You're a good battle tactician, Dunneal, but truly you need a king to manage a war."

"I don't understand, sir," Dunneal said.

"Coronation is merely the inevitable first step," Sarthius said. "I do nothing without purpose. You must think beyond the battle and consider what our navy – the navy of a united Veraland – can accomplish on a broader scale. That is, if you wish to keep the position you have been promised."

"Aye sir," Dunneal said. "I will endeavor toward readiness as my highest priority."

"Vindrel, you have your ship."

"Understood, sire," Vindrel said. "They won't escape me."

"They?" Dunneal said.

"She had help besides the witch," Vindrel said. "I think I know who, based on my contacts."

"We're checking every ship that leaves," Dunneal said. "Nothing that floats is getting out without a thorough inspection."

"They're already gone," Vindrel said. "Out into the dry highlands. But don't worry. Their options are limited. We'll find them."

Sarthius glanced back at the cleric. "Ah, Claire, you may leave now, if this scene does not suit you."

"Thank you, my li – your highness," Claire corrected herself.

"Oh," Sarthius said. "I have another stipend for your daughter's studies." He reached in his pocket and drew forth a small bag.

Claire looked at Vindrel, who seemed not to react. The bag, made of burlap and topped with a simple string, sat in Sarthius's palm.

My daughter. Marriage and children were not permitted for the devotees of Verbus, the priesthood that managed the church itself, serving as clergy to all other clergymen. The Church of the Twelve was the source of all knowledge in Deideron, and indeed the world, for beyond the divine strand and the fractured North the land seemed to be filled with warring savages: men who had forgotten the light of the Twelve Gods and their gifts, and people whose humanity was in real doubt – remnants of the old races.

Claire's daughter Maribel was the result of her failing at being neutral with the nobility – failing to uphold her oaths. The girl's father had been a prince in the warring kingdoms of the divine strand, the remnants of the last great holy empire, and that put her at great risk of harm from competitors to the eleven thrones. She had managed to enroll her daughter in a devotion path to Nostera, the goddess of healing, much younger than would normally be allowed, in order to keep her hidden away. This she kept a secret to all, even the girl's father, but Sarthius had known about Maribel almost as soon as she had accepted a position as minister in Cataling. Somehow, the count knew everything.

He had come to her offering charity in the form of an educational stipend, but she understood what it truly was: a threat, and the sort of threat that keeps a woman up at night. Knowledge was part of his power, and that knowledge had been well-used against Claire. With her connections in the church, she had caused several key members of the nobility to be exiled as apostates, all with mysteriously sharp drawings of guilt and evidence of which Sarthius seemed always to know.

Maribel needs this.

Claire stepped forward to take the bag. At that moment, she saw, as if slowed in time, Ardala the servant girl being thrown naked onto the bonfire in the courtyard below. It seemed like she could not look away as a scream escaped her mouth. She felt her fingers clutching the bag, but turning away from the execution seemed impossible. Vaguely she felt Sarthius's spider-like fingers around her wrist, holding her. Flesh blackened as smoke and flame enveloped the count's victim. Silence in the crowd answered the woman's tortured cries.

The bag of gunpowder around the woman's neck finally exploded, ending her pain in a flash of fire and blood. Sarthius pulled Claire close and whispered with hot, sickly breath in her ear. It was like the hissing of a snake.

"Power. Remember."

I: DRY HIGHLANDS

The stars stand blinking cold as winter frost
The constellations frozen overhead
Within the portal I'm forever lost
Through pathless wilderness I'm blindly led

Charlotte opened her eyes to see the firmament standing strong, with the moon in the west of the sky, barely peeking over the edge of the ancient wall. She was wrapped tightly in the wool cloak, and the fire still smoldered warm in the hearth, but she was alone. The song and voice faded, sucked into the wind, which whistled through the gaps in the walls, where the mortar that joined the ancient stones together had worn to dust and blown away. It sounded to her like a penny whistle and a voice at once, shrill and yet somehow melodious, blending with the song she heard even as it drowned the words. She drew the patched cloak closer around her body, wondering how much worse the wind would be outside the ruins of the old house.

The stars looked strange and alien to her, unfamiliar in their place where the roof of the house had once been. She realized it had been years since she really observed them.

Rone's voice returned:

Ten years have come and gone outside on earth
By fate, not chance, I do at last return
With time enough to contemplate your worth

He entered through a gap in the walls that was once a door and saw her looking at him. His voice cracked. "How are you doing?" he said, clearing his throat. He bent down by the fire and began rummaging in his backpack.

"I feel like I'm either dreaming, or waking from a dream," Charlotte said. She coughed softly. Rone turned his head and raised an eyebrow at her. "What's that look about?"

Rone chuckled softly as he removed a small copper pot from his bag. "Well, you didn't really answer my question, did you?"

"I thought I did," Charlotte grumbled.

"Were you dreaming? Dreams are more powerful up here." He emptied a waterskin into the pot and put it on the coals of one side of the fire. Rone leaned back against the stones of what had once been the central hearth of the house. He opened up a small bag and withdrew some herbs, which he crushed with his hands and emptied into the pot.

"I don't understand."

Rone picked up something else – something he had gone out to fetch that Charlotte couldn't remember the name of – and put it in the pot as well. He sat down by the hearth and stirred the pot with the end of a dagger, his sole eating implement after Charlotte had lost his fork days earlier.

"What were you dreaming about?"

Charlotte pulled the blanket up to disguise a sudden warmth in her cheeks. "Forget I said anything."

Rone laughed. "Not possible. You can tell me."

Charlotte hesitated. "Dragons."

Rone suddenly looked at her with wide eyes. "Really? That would be quite an omen." He watched Charlotte for a long moment, then turned back to the pot. "No. Something embarrassing, then. Don't worry about it. Just remember that dreams have power, especially in a place like this." He looked around. "It's like you can feel the remnants of the Prim, lapping against the stones. Now, how are you doing – are you feeling sick?"

"I'm doing fine," Charlotte said. "Loads better, actually."

"You were red as a gill and unable to speak just a few hours ago."

"It's just…" Charlotte swallowed hard. Her throat felt like she had swallowed nettles. "I… get sick sometimes."

Rone stood up. "Then we ought to be off. We're behind the schedule I had imagined, but if we make up for most of the day you spent groaning and sleeping, we may yet arrive in Masala ahead of… whoever Catannel paid to hunt you."

Charlotte sighed and pushed herself up, feeling the wind drive up the spine of her loose blouse, opened up just hours earlier when she thought she would roast to death. She shivered and her elbows shook.

"You're flushed." Rone strode over and put a hand on her forehead. "Why the lies?"

"It's not a lie."

Rone went back to the pot and dipped a cup into it. He held it up and blew steam off of the top, then carefully walked back to Charlotte.

"This will break the fever," he said, holding the cup to her lips.

Charlotte shut her mouth tightly in response, drawing it to a thin line.

"Come on," Rone said. "I went through a lot of trouble to fetch the proper mushroom and herbs for this."

Charlotte shook her head silently, like an obstinate child.

Rone sat back on his haunches with a sigh. "Do you want me to drink it?" He took a sip from the cup and smiled. "I wouldn't take you all the way out here just to poison you."

Charlotte swallowed painfully again. "Where did you learn that?"

Rone shrugged.

"You're not a physician," she said.

"I'm not pretending to be one. Are you getting religious on me?"

"I thought *you* were the religious one."

Rone shrugged again.

"It's sorcery, isn't it? Magic? A potion?" Her eyes grew wide. "A magic potion."

Rone chuckled. His face straightened and he looked around. "It's all sorcery. Or was. All of this is just the remnants of what once was magic – the eternal dream that persisted and became the mundane."

"I don't want any part of your magic."

"You have a part of it whether you want it or not," Rone said. "This little sickness you have is magic, a leftover of malevolence, more ancient than we can comprehend, made real. Or, I assume so."

Charlotte shook her head. "I wouldn't have come had I known you were a sorcerer."

"Oh, I think you would have," Rone said. "But I'm not a sorcerer. Or a wizard, or any other such fanciful distinction. If I was, I wouldn't have needed to drag you through the dry highlands, and I wouldn't bother fetching herbs to ease your body. I would just… conjure a spell and cure you, or blast my way onto a boat, and pilot it with phantoms." He laughed, but Charlotte stared at him with a deep frown. "Please drink it. I promise it will make you feel better. Besides, you're already as much as an apostate now. Might as well use a bit of magic."

Charlotte nodded and took the hot liquid he offered. It was bitter and burned going down, and sat in her stomach in a queasy sort of way. She drank all of it, not because she trusted Rone, but because she finally resigned herself once again to being helpless.

"Now rest while you can," Rone said. "I'm going to catch a few winks whilst I can, then I'll see if I can shoot us some breakfast. I saw some sign of rabbits while I was looking for those herbs."

Rone put out his bedroll next to Charlotte, with the hot side of the hearth facing both of them.

The wind died down a little, and Charlotte could hear crickets.

"What was that you were singing?" she said, pushing herself up on her elbows.

"Nothing," he said. "Just a song my mother used to sing to herself. It's part of an old story. Very old. I guess I was feeling a bit nostalgic. I didn't mean to wake you. You were pretty out of it."

"Would you sing the rest for me?"

"I'm not much of a singer."

"I thought it was lovely. You should hear me play the cello sometime, then you wouldn't be so self-conscious."

"Maybe some other time, when I have the words." He tapped his temple and nodded. "Let's hope for dragons, eh?"

*

The day was bright when Charlotte awoke. Rone was building up the fire, roasting on a spit the remains of what she assumed was once a rabbit. He noticed her stirring and shuffled over, picking up a cup on the way.

"Another dose, before the fever returns," he said, holding the cup to her lips. She drank it. It tasted much worse cold, but feeling tolerable for the first time in more than a day, she let Rone give her the whole thing in one draught.

"Thank you," she said, gasping after the drink.

"You're welcome. It's better in one gulp, by the way." He winked. "I'll have breakfast ready shortly."

Charlotte looked around, watching the trees above the roofless house dance in the breeze, dark green leaves fluttering and rustling loudly.

"What is this place, anyway?"

"An old farmstead."

"Is there a village nearby?"

"No," Rone said. "Just ruins like this. There won't be much in the way of people till we're coming out of the highlands."

"I wonder who lived here."

"The inscription on the hearth says *Molney*." Rone pointed to a large stone lining what remained of the central hearth. Charlotte crawled forward to inspect it. It was a black stone, weathered and rough, but the inscription remained chiseled clearly, as if that part of the stone was immune to the passage of rain and wind. It was of a series of angled letters that she did not recognize.

"You can read this?"

"Aye. It's an old version of the runes, but the phonetics are easy enough."

"All those letters to say 'Molney'?"

"Not quite." Rone pointed to the top line. "That's an old verse about… well, the *verse* and the *inverse*. The mundane and the changeable. An archaic version of the old tongue, but readable."

"A line about magic, then," Charlotte said.

"You could say that. Now, at least. The verse is the power of the dream, the power to make reality what you wish it to be. The inverse is the reality that already exists. The limitations of the physical. Traditionally, you must know both, and balance both, for prosperity and achievement. The inscription technically reads, *Know the inverse to become who you are, know the verse to become who you were meant to be.* The line below is the name Molney."

"I wonder who they were, or where they went."

"My guess is that they went the way of all the others. Went down to the coast and abandoned the old ways. Didn't produce children, or the community produced too few children to defend itself in later generations. A loremaster might know the history of the family, but the last one in Veraland disappeared after the war with Marcus Grantel."

"Marcus killed the last loremaster?"

"No, the loremaster *disappeared,* along with all that remained of the Southern Clans – the Bitterwheats, Buckleys, and Ironshoes. Maybe others."

Charlotte narrowed her eyes as she got closer to the fire. "What do you mean they *disappeared?*"

Rone shrugged and smirked. "Well, I can't say except that Marcus couldn't find them. The farmhouses were all deserted, the livestock set free or gone - not that such an ending to his purge is widely known."

"You don't know where they all went?"

"You ask a lot of questions."

"What else am I supposed to do? I didn't bring any books."

Rone nodded. "Good point." He turned the meat over, exposing dripping flesh to the fire. "No, I don't know where they went. I wasn't there and I didn't know them. My clan kept to itself until the end."

"What happened to your family?"

Rone was silent for a few moments. After a stretch, he took the rabbit off the fire and began cutting flesh from the spit and handing it to Charlotte, who ate each piece as it was delivered. It was tough, but rich and satisfying, well-seasoned with hunger.

Rone took a deep breath. "My family dwindled. I was the first to abandon my village, but there were few of us left at that point."

Charlotte ate in silence for a few moments.

"I think this place is nice."

"We can't stay here, if that's what you are thinking. They'll come here eventually. Vindrel will know I've come this way once they figure out that we couldn't have taken a ship."

"Who?"

Rone bit his lip. "The captain of the guard. He's bound to be the hound set after us. He's a shrewd man. A clever man."

"Cleverer than you?"

Rone chuckled. "Not by a long shot." Rone looked around. "And far less imaginative."

***

Rone lowered his spyglass and looked at Charlotte, who was leaning in against a large half-dead bush.

"The city is closed," he said, rolling into a sitting position behind the large, wind-smooth boulder.

"What do you mean? I can see it from here."

"The hamlets, yes, but not the city itself. Look past and you can see the old wall. There are lines in all the entrances."

"So, they beat us here?"

"It could be something else. Masala is built on the slave trade, and trouble is constant. Maybe a little revolt." He wiped the sweat from his brow and scratched at his dirty neck. "Though, it's probably best to assume that Vindrel has sailed round the Isle before we could walk it."

"Assume the worst?"

Rone gave her a half-smile. "The worst? Oh, my dear, there are far worse things than that. It's just fairly likely. We should operate under that assumption."

"Where do we go now? Taisafeld? Some other town on the south coast?"

Rone shook his head. "We've already delayed too long, and our best chance for passage to the Northmarch, or hell, any-where on the mainland, is the Silver City."

"So, we're in the same predicament as Cataling." Charlotte pushed herself up to look over the crest. She could just make out, past the walled city, the ocean. "Only now we're tired and dirty."

"Not at all," Rone said. "Well, we certainly are dirty. Catannel doesn't rule here. He has no authority over House Harec. Not yet, anyway. And I have contacts I can exploit within the city. We just have to get over the walls."

"Over?" Charlotte said, giving Rone an incredulous look.

"Or through the gate. We can't just walk in, though."

"So, what are we going to do?"

Rone impulsively examined one of his pistols, shaking his head. "I'll think of something. Let's rest a bit, then we can move off back up the coastal road; maybe find a group to blend in with."

*

Charlotte watched from the reeds, pointing Rone's musket down toward her feet and hoping she didn't have to shoulder it. It was alien in her hands, though not because of its firing mechanism, which had been banned. She had held – and shot – muskets many times in her life, but it had been so long, and the person she was when she last held a gun was so divorced from her current mind, that it felt like something new and terrible that could turn on her.

The man Rone had decided was their mark stirred from where he squatted relieving himself.

He never saw the tall and lean man approaching from behind, nor would he have been able to put up a fight if he did, stuck in his most vulnerable position. He had only the rustle of the bushes behind him to warn him, but his nerves were slow.

Rone had his hand around the man's neck before he could even turn his head to look, and his dagger pierced his lung so swiftly the man could only kick out with one leg before he lost his will and was pushed down to the ground.

Rone held him firm for a few seconds, then his kicking ceased.

The body rolled over to the side and, though she knew there wasn't life in the eyes of the haggard victim, Charlotte was sure he was looking at her.

She dropped the gun and stood up, feeling vomit coming. She fought it back for a few moments, but still ended up loudly throwing up part of her lunch.

Rone padded through the mud toward her, wiping his blade on a dirty cloth, frowning in a kind of accusation.

"Sorry," Charlotte choked.

"Quiet." He touched her shoulders and pushed her back down into the mound of grasses.

They heard a female scream a few moments later.

"One of his slaves," Rone said. "Come on."

"I need a moment," Charlotte said. She swallowed back more bile.

"He's not worth thinking on," Rone said.

"How can you not think on it?"

"I'm a professional. It's my job not to think on it. What else did you hire me for?"

Charlotte felt tears threatening to spring from the corners of her eyes. "Not this."

"It is done. We can only move forward. I need you to trust me."

Charlotte took a breath and nodded.

Names," Tugg said through clenched teeth, his one eye still running over the notes on his dirty ledger. The gate he managed marked one of the smallest portals into the walled city of Masala, relegated mostly to foot traffic and pack mules. The stone archway, hiding a strong iron gate, was moss-covered and reeked slightly of a perpetual moisture.

"Munin." the man in front of Tugg said, his heavy boots squishing through the mud that had been tracked over the city cobbles. His dark hair hung wet about his shoulders, and his cloak was nearly soaked. "This is my sister, Daera." He stuck his thumb out at the woman beside him, who wore a large-brimmed hat that obscured her eyes. A gun of some sort lay cradled in her arms, wrapped in a sheath of leather against the rain. Both of them were covered in dust and grit that had turned to a grey silt in the rain and dripped from the corners of their long coats.

Tugg dipped his pen into his inkwell. "What about her?" He pointed the pen past the pair at a short girl with hair that might once have been blonde. Tugg pegged her at about twenty, but a hard-lived twenty. Iron cuffs rattled on her wrists.

"She's a slave, here for market. I thought it best her master give her a proper name," the man said.

"Selling your village-mates, eh? Things must be getting on badly on the floodplain," Tugg said, shifting his nearly dissolved coca leaf to the other side of his mouth and clenching it tightly.

"Mind your own business," the woman said. She frowned and turned away, looking over her shoulder at some horses milling outside the gate.

Tugg hummed a deep chuckle to himself. Insults always gave you a better idea of who a person was than niceties.

"Why is the city shut?" Munin said, his tone neutral. "I've never been stopped at a gate in peacetime before."

Tugg grinned. "The gate is *my* business, not yours. Now I need names for *all* of you."

Munin looked back at the slave, his yellow-green eyes hard, and nodded to her.

The young woman looked at the man holding her chains for a moment, then shouted, "They killed my master and stole me! They're murderers!" She rushed forward, then found herself falling into the mud as Munin tugged on her chains. He pulled her up by her wrists, easily hoisting her face up to the level of his chest.

"Blast me, but don't make me tear you up before we even get you to market!" he said, his eyes wide with rage. His companion put her wrapped gun above her head, as if she was going to slam the butt into the slave's face. The slave twisted away and whimpered.

"It's true!" the slave screamed.

"Slaves will say anything to get out of their debts," the woman said, still holding the butt of the long gun high.

"Call her Hella," Munin said, staring into Tugg's one eye.

Tugg paused as he was writing and chewed on his lip, unsure if he should follow his gut.

"What is it?" the man said.

"I'll need to have a look at your gun."

"The good count having problems with the church?"

"What's the hold-up?!" Another man shouted from behind the trio. He held the reins of a laden mule, his simple clothing soaked through.

"My job is my own," Tugg said. "If I want to inspect your gun, I get to, unless you want to take the round way up to the

- 22 -

West gate and lose half the day, and deal with fellas that are much sourer than I am. Now, unwrap that iron."

The slavemasters looked to each other and then nodded. Hesitantly, Daera untied a small thong and slipped the gun out of the leather, displaying a simple stock and bare iron receiver. Tugg looked closely at it.

"If this is a matchlock, I'm a dead rabbit," he said, looking at the vacant screw holes on the gun's receiver.

"It's legal," Munin said.

"I'll be the judge of that," Tugg said.

"Tugg! What are you doing you old fool?" Michel, one of the lieutenants of the guard, rode up to the old arch and reined in his horse.

"My job," Tugg said, and spit out a discolored wad of coca onto the ground.

"Are these them, or not?" Michel said.

Tugg's one eye looked over Munin and the slave. "No. I'd say not."

"Then let them through," Michel said. "You're backing things up."

"They're in the slave trade."

"I don't give a damn what trade they're in. We have orders. If they ain't the ones we're looking for, send them on through."

"Aye."

"Aye what?"

"Aye, *sir*," Tugg said, and put his hand to his chest as a salute.

"That's better. You have the morning ledgers?"

Tugg nodded and pulled his current piece of paper from his wooden ledger stand, then handed it to the armored lieutenant. Michel quickly rolled it up and stuck it in a saddlebag, then rode off.

"We'll be off then," Munin said, stepping forward. Tugg put a hand out.

"Just a moment. You interested in a private sale?" he nodded to the slave, being all but dragged by Munin. "Avoid the auction cut. I know a richer or two that might have a taste for what you've got."

"I'm taking her to market," Munin replied.

Tugg scowled. "Alright, move along." He watched the trio slip away and stuck another coca leaf in his cheek, then looked at his ledger. He realized he had forgotten to write their names down. "Who were they?" he said to himself. He shook his head and dipped the quill into his inkwell, then wrote down what he could remember. "No matter."

*

Rone and Charlotte shuffled out of the crowded gateway and into an open thoroughfare, dragging the slave girl between them. The girl's dress, once a light-colored slip now darkened to a muddy brown by abuse and weather, clung to her thighs as she stumbled behind. Despite the rain, the tenements that crowded the south wall of Masala felt hot and stuffy, and smoke from brick chimneys blended with the sky, making the clouds appear only head high. The sea was close, but from the feel of the air, nobody there would have known it. They followed a winding path, away from the gate and through a slum.

"Here," Rone said, and pulled both Charlotte and the slave into a narrow alleyway. A dog, emaciated and frightful, looked up at them from where it rummaged through a pile of refuse. It ran away as they pushed past, stopping to stare at them from a stair step where the alley ended.

"You're gonna get it," the slave said.

"Quiet," Rone said, and removed a tall satchel from the inside of his tattered coat. He undid a leather cord around it and opened it, revealing a row of metal tools. He pulled out a few bent pieces of scrap: a rake and flat wrench. "Sit down." He pointed at the ground. The slave girl looked up into his hard, yellow-green eyes and sat down quickly, the dirty dress pulling back to reveal legs that looked shining white compared to the road grit that covered her bare arms and shins.

"Why are we stopping here?" Charlotte said. She looked at the entrance to the alley nervously.

"Cutting loose the baggage," Rone said. He put the flattened wrench into the large lock on the slave girl's shackles and quickly began raking through its two tumblers. "Wish I'd bothered finding the key." A few seconds later, the first shackle fell away and landed in the alley with a dull thud.

"What are you doing?" the slave asked.

"I'm setting you free. What does it look like?" Rone said.

"Marcos has brothers on the road behind him," the girl said, holding up her other wrist. "They'll be looking for me when they find his body - and for you."

"I'm quite good at not being found," Rone said. He picked the lock on the second shackle. The girl rubbed her wrists, which were flaking and covered with mild iron sores.

"What now?" the girl said.

"You run, and stay hidden, and do whatever you will with your life," Rone said. "Consider it my thanks for helping us through the gates."

"That's it?"

"Maybe I'm getting soft and I should just kill you, eh?" He flashed the girl a grim smile.

"What about this?" The girl said. She pulled up the dingy sleeve of her dress and revealed a brand of two letters.

"They branded a woman?" Charlotte said.

Rone tilted his head. "Odd."

"It's barbaric, doing that to a woman," Charlotte said.

"It's likely she ran away a few times," Rone said. "Well, nothing I can do about that. Not here, anyway. I might recommend you find a friend with a hot iron to stamp it out. Won't be very fun." Rone flinched as Charlotte shoved a folded piece of paper into his arms. "What's this?"

"Title papers," Charlotte said. "I found them in her owner's bags. We could have her cleared."

"I'm not much on forgeries. Even if I was, we don't have the time." Rone handed the paper to the slave, who turned it over, wondering. "I'm sure you can find someone to forge a clerk's stamp for a modest sum."

"You don't know anyone?" Charlotte said. She lifted her head and locked her clear, almost tearful eyes on Rone.

"No," Rone said, and looked away. He stepped past the slave and grasped Charlotte's arm. "Let's keep moving."

"Wait," Charlotte said. She knelt by the slave girl and pulled from a pouch at her waist a handful of silver coins. "Take this. It should be enough to get you started. New clothes, a few days' worth of meals-"

"Try a few months!" the girl said, her eyes widening as the coins fell into her palms.

Rone scoffed audibly and Charlotte turned back to give him a frown.

"Fine," Rone said. He looked at the slave. "There's a man that goes by the name of Getty, a few streets away from the docks in a book shop. If he charges you more than twenty cyprals for a forgery, he's cheating you." He looked at Charlotte. "Let's go. *Now.*"

Charlotte cast a last look at the slave girl, gave a half-hearted smile, then jogged after Rone as he exited the alleyway and joined in the throng of people traveling the city on their morning business. She pulled up beside him, trying her best to match his long, swift stride.

Quietly he spoke, "If you wake up to a dagger in your belly tonight, remember that it was your kindness that brought it on."

"We couldn't just leave her like that," Charlotte said back loudly.

"Shh!" Rone said. He continued quietly, his voice holding a hint of voiced anger, "Yes, we could. Turning her loose was enough. It would keep her owner's brothers off of us and earn plenty of gratitude from the girl. Now you've shown her coin. Not just a pinch of copper to get supper, either, but nearly as much as she would have been sold for. Enough to really matter."

"That was the point. With that and a little smarts, she could have a real life."

"It was foolish. Urchins talk to other urchins. We throw away silver like that, she'll know we have gold. She's a slave. Don't think for a moment she won't fall in with a pimp or worse here. Eyes and ears will be searching for that money. For us."

Charlotte cast her eyes down and thrust her hands into her pockets. "I'm sorry."

Rone sighed audibly. "What's done is done, and I'm a part of it myself. Come on."

*

The western part of Masala was higher in elevation than the tenements, allowing a steady breeze off the sea in the afternoon to blow through Charlotte and Rone's long coats. The streets were mostly deserted, and the people that did walk down either side of the paved avenues were moderately well-dressed; men wore waistcoats more often than plain shirts, and women bustled dresses more often than aprons. Rone and Charlotte, with their dirty long coats and packs, stood out among the colorfully dressed citizenry, catching glances from passers-by busy enough to spare little else. Charlotte realized she was a woman wearing trousers, an uncommon if not alluring sight on the Isle of Veraland.

Rone walked quickly ahead of her, continuing the long, protracted silence that had settled between them when they entered the city. On their journey to Masala, through the dry highlands of the Isle where men were a rarer sight than beasts, the silence between conversations had been comfortable to Charlotte. Somehow, in the crowded city, the lack of talk was maddening.

"Where are we going?" Charlotte said, daring to break the silence.

Rone turned his head slightly to look at her. "Somewhere to stay. Out of the way of the bustle. Normally, I'd choose something a bit shadier, but given the interchange with the slave, we'll have to do with accommodations that are actually decent." Rone flashed a slight smile.

"You? In places that are actually decent?" Charlotte smiled back

"*Merely* decent," Rone said. "I shall do my best to condescend to your preferred level of comfort, though I fear I might undo weeks of work and spoil you to hard living forever. A warm bed will do little to make you long for the road, which I suspect we'll see more of before the end."

Charlotte sighed. "A bed. Dreamer! I feel like I can scarcely remember the pleasure."

Rone turned his head again, his brow furrowed. "Careful who you invoke. Folks in decent places don't appreciate blasphemy, even in an off-hand way. We get enough looks as it is."

Charlotte nodded. She wanted to say sorry again, but some degree of pride held her back. "I've just spent too much time with you. It seems I'm starting to pick up your way of speaking."

"I can tell. Invoke a different god while you're here." Rone turned away and picked up the pace again, leading Charlotte up a wide avenue. They turned down a slightly narrower street, lined with shops and boarding houses that stood several stories tall, the masonry and tile roofs clean despite being ancient. Rone paused in front of an inn, the wooden sign above the door waving slightly in the breeze.

"The Sevelny Inn," Charlotte said, reading the sign and looking at the closed, simply carved doors.

"The proprietor's name," Rone said, digging around in one of his side bags, which rested under his powder horn.

"Not very creative."

"That's exactly what we want. Here." Rone nodded toward a narrow alley and walked briskly down it. Charlotte followed close behind. Her pack scraped against the side of the building, filling her ears with an odd echo. Around the corner was the rear entrance of the inn and a small porch. A door stood open to the kitchen, airing out the morning's cooking. A black cast-iron pipe from the stove stuck out of a window, a few wisps of smoke escaping from its capped top and curling through the still air of the alleyway.

"Stay here," Rone said. "I'll come get you shortly." Charlotte nodded.

Rone walked back out of the alley swiftly. After he disappeared, Charlotte let herself draw a long breath and a sigh. She looked around at the darkened backs of the stores and houses, each going down a straight line to streets that looked bright in the dim alley. A small refuse pile stood behind the inn's kitchen, full of old bones and other discarded fragments of food. Charlotte could see movement that she imagined to be a rat rummaging inside, and it made her scrunch her nose up.

She backed up to the corner and took off her pack. She rubbed her shoulders softly, feeling the ache of the burden fade. She had become used to the weight of it after so many days on the road, but the pain reminded her often that such things were still new to her. With that in mind, she thought back to her first days on the road and smiled. Then, she'd been scarcely able to shoulder anything; now, she could carry her weight. Charlotte had grown strong in a relatively short time, and that gave her a bit of hope.

She started slightly when Rone stepped out of the kitchen door and looked about.

"There you are," he said. "I got us a room upstairs, with a view of the street. Come on."

Charlotte picked her bag back up and slung it over a single shoulder, then followed Rone into the kitchen, currently deserted except for a dog lying in the corner, moving only his eyes. Just past the tight arrangements of stoves and ovens was a narrow stairwell.

"There's a rat in the alley," Charlotte whispered at the dog. As she passed. "Go get him!"

The dog raised its head, long ears drooping over its head, and looked out the back door, as if thinking it over in his own mind. He dropped his head back down, as if he had decided the rat was not worth the effort.

*

The sun had come through the clouds in the west, bathing the tidy inn room in warm light and illuminating the grit that had worked into Charlotte's hair over the many miles between Cataling and Masala. The window was open, hinting at a breeze that could not be properly felt in the land-facing room. It was humid in the so-called Silver City, and Charlotte continued to sweat even with her jacket removed.

She sat and worked at the tangles in her long, copper-red hair. It pegged her as a foreigner in Veraland, where even the occasional blonde shock among a sea of brown drew stares, and so Charlotte, at the bidding of Rone, had twisted it into a braid and stuffed it down the back of her long jacket, then covered her head with Rone's oversized hat. Her hairbrush, an ornate thing with tortoise-shell inlay and stiff boar bristles, found the knots in the hair all too well, but she was still glad to tend it, letting it remind her of her womanhood.

"I can't wait for a bath," she said to herself.

The door squeaked slightly as it opened a crack. When Rone did not appear, Charlotte felt a sudden surge of panic. She dropped her hairbrush on the ground and looked around for Rone's pistol. It was nowhere.

"It's me," the voice of Rone said.

"Come in. I'm decent."

The door fell all the way open and Rone entered, carrying two plates filled with freshly roasted chicken and bread along one arm. He kicked the door closed behind him and rushed over to the little table beside the open window, where he deposited the plates hastily.

"I figured a little bit of hot food should be first on the agenda," Rone said, smiling slightly. He pulled a bundle of knives and forks from his jacket pocket and dumped them on the table. Charlotte picked her hairbrush back up off the floor and put it on the windowsill, then pushed her chair closer to the table.

"I can't remember the last time I had a hot meal," she said. She picked up a fork and examined it, then wiped some of the dust off on one of the few clean spots left on her cotton shirt.

"I can," Rone said, tearing apart the quarter of a chicken on his plate. He took a bite and chewed in satisfaction for a moment. "I cooked us rabbit. It was at the old Molney homestead."

"It was just an expression. I do remember." She smiled as she carefully carved the chicken into neat slices. "I can't believe I ate rabbit. Disgusting."

"You didn't think so at the time," Rone said. He took a hearty bite from one of the bread rolls, then said while chewing. "Hunger really is the finest seasoning."

"My mother would have a fit watching me eat a fresh-skinned rabbit. Or this." She put one of the chicken slices into her mouth and chewed.

"What's wrong with chicken?"

Charlotte swallowed. "This is cooked all wrong. Pot roasting a chicken is a sin, and with this much salt such a deed is practically criminal."

"It's an old bird. You can't throw an old bird on a hot fire and expect to be able to chew it," Rone said.

"No, you can't." She shrugged. "I suppose this really isn't that bad." Charlotte took another bite.

"Aye, but is it as good as the rabbit?"

"Of course not." She smiled at him. "A servant came by earlier. A young girl. They have a few baths downstairs."

"You answered the door?" Rone said. He held a forkful of chicken in front of his face as if his hand had frozen there.

"It was a girl, couldn't have been more than twelve. Anyway, I decided to have a bath drawn."

Rone dropped his fork. "Damn it, girl. We're not on vacation here."

"I need a bath."

"It's not about the bath. The innkeeper thinks I'm here alone. Didn't you think about why I brought you in through the back? Eyes are watching!"

"We're in Masala, not Cataling, like you said."

"A Masala with the gates shut. Dreamer! Do you ever spare a thought to the danger you're in?"

Charlotte sat silent for a moment, then said. "You ordered two plates of food, mister clever. Did you spare a thought to that?"

"I told the cook I was extra hungry. It's not unheard of."

"So hungry you needed two sets of silverware?"

"Bah," Rone said. He began shoveling food into his mouth at an accelerated rate. His mouth half-full, he said, "I'll drop some hints that we're eloping or having an affair or something. The most believable lies are the ones you spend effort covering up."

"Then it's settled. We'll have baths."

"Fine." He looked up at her. "I suppose it will make us look a little less road-worn. A little more like we fit in. We should dye your hair. Maybe cut it too." He dug back into his food.

Charlotte held her hair up in the light. "I suppose you're right." She sighed.

"Something wrong?"

"Just a woman's vanity."

"It'll grow back." Rone paused and looked at her, his face casting creases of sadness. "Which is a good thing, of course."

III: Farthow

What ya think, cap'n?" Colby said. He pushed the scabbard to his rapier to the side and took a knee beside the woman. Her eyes were closed, and her hair was a mess of tangles that obscured most of her face. Lying in her outstretched hand was a pipe, with a half-burnt pill of opium still stuck in the bowl. Colby pushed her hair away, revealing a dirt-streaked young woman. A rough tunic covered her upper arms and chest, but she was bare below the waist.

"Looks like her," Farthow said. He scratched absent-mindedly at the place where his short-cut blonde beard met the high collar of his green jacket.

"First thing she did was hit the smack, eh?" Colby said. He pushed the woman onto her back. He legs fell apart, and still, she did not wake. Colby, almost analytically, examined her genitals with his gloved right hand.

"Second thing," Farthow said. "A friend of mine forged papers for her earlier today."

"Looks like somebody had his way with her."

Farthow spat onto the dirty wooden floor. "Figures. You can't expect much different if you're a woman in a place like this."

"Pretty much what she would have expected if she'd been sold though, eh?"

"I suppose." Farthow kicked the pipe out of the woman's hands. "The smell of this place makes me sick."

"Captain, I found the keeper." Farthow turned as Dem entered, his rifle held lightly in one hand. The young man pushed his dark hair up out of his eyes as he looked at the woman on the floor, legs splayed open.

"Well?" Farthow said, raising an eyebrow to his young sergeant.

Dem tore his eyes away from the girl and looked to Farthow. "I shook him down and found a cache of silver. More than she could have spent on opium." He reached in his pocket and withdrew a handful of coins. "Odd marks."

"Let me see," Farthow said, and took one of the silver coins from Dem's palm. Colby stood up beside him to look. "This is an argent from Northmarch. Brulia."

"I don't recognize the face," Colby said.

"That's because he's been dead at least a century," Farthow said. "Vaslius." Farthow picked up another coin. "This one's from Hviterland."

"Does that mean something to you?" Dem said.

"To me, yes," Farthow said, and handed the coins back to Dem. "To you, not so much. I want both of you to turn this house out. Find every coin. If it has a mint mark to the Isle, you can keep it. All others surrender to me. Do not make me mistrust you."

"Aye," Dem said, and nodded to Colby. "What about her?"

"I'll try to get her up and clothed," Farthow said. "You may have to help me cart her back to the castle. Once she sobers up, we'll figure out what to do with her."

"You going to give her back to her owner?" Colby said.

Farthow shook his head. He knelt down and pulled a folded and piece of paper from a pile of clothes nearby. "She's got free papers."

"You said they were a forgery," Colby said.

"I did. Now turn this place out. Throw the keeper out too. Go."

Colby and Dem stepped past him and out into the hall of the opium den. Farthow sighed and looked at the woman, still drifting in an opium trance. He closed her legs and pulled her faded skirt over her nakedness. "Well Hella, if that is any true name of yours," he said softly, "I must keep you away from prying eyes, since you are so unwilling to do it yourself. Hopefully, you don't resent me too much for the cage."

*

"Ah, here he is now," Drath Harec said. "Welcome back, Captain Bitterwheat."

"Aye, lord," Farthow said and bowed low, stopping among his long strides for just a moment before quickly approaching the count of Masala and his guest.

"This is captain Stonefield," Harec said, gesturing to the burly man standing beside him on the wide balcony. The man wore a green jacket similar to Farthow's, but with dark grey pants. "He's Cataling's captain of the guard. And a highland man."

"Pleased to meet you, sir Stonefield," Farthow said.

"Vindrel will do." The burly man extended a hand, which Farthow shook.

"Sorry for the delay, lord," Farthow said. "My men came across an opium den, and we felt compelled to turn it out."

"I trust you burned the opium," Harec said, almost absentmindedly. He looked down at the intricate gold-threaded embroidery of his own state jacket.

"Of course, lord. Not a trace was left. I'm having a clerk make up the deed to the place for an auction."

"Good, good," Harec said. "Now, mister Bitterwheat, the captain here is on a mission from Count Catannel, searching for a pair of fugitives. I told him you would provide him with full support."

"Um, yes, of course, sir," Farthow said, his eyes widening. "What sort of support does he need?"

"I could use a cadre of men who know the city," Vindrel said. "I'm looking for a man and a woman. The woman has light red hair. We need her at least alive for trial. The man… well, I prefer to have him alive too. He would be a good source of information for me."

"Their crimes?" Farthow said.

"Treason, apparently," Harec said.

"I see," Farthow said. "Well, I shall set myself to providing you with some good men from the guard straight away."

"No need for such a rush," Harec said. "Why don't we all have a glass of wine? I would be very interested to hear of the goings-on in Cataling. Reports from the other cities have been sparse since the death of the king."

"With all due respect and honor, my lord," Vindrel said, "I would not feel right reclining and enjoying the pleasure of wine, and your company, without seeing to my duties."

Harec sighed. "I understand, captain. Perhaps you will share a glass with me when you apprehend your quarry?"

Vindrel bowed. "I would be honored, lord."

Farthow looked to Vindrel. "I'll collect my men and send them down to the courtyard."

"Thank you," Vindrel said with a nod. "And you, my lord." He bowed and stepped out of the balcony.

Harec watched him disappear into the hallway, then said. "Is there a man or two you can trust?"

"I trust Dem, but we'll have to let him in on things. Colby I'd want to keep in the dark."

"Very well, Dem it shall be. Any luck so far?"

Farthow handed Harec a silver coin, stamped with a large bearded head and set of crossed spears on the reverse.

Harec raised an eyebrow. "A Hviterland argent. Interesting."

"One of several."

"You have them already?" Harec fingered the coin in his hand.

"No, but I have a slave that was with them briefly. Her tongue should be loosened shortly."

"Keep her locked up and away from Vindrel. I want these fugitives delivered to *me*. Under no circumstances should they be returned to Cataling. Keep them from Vindrel at any costs, do you understand me?"

"Of course, lord. I shall see it done. I am already gathering leads."

***

Rone could hear the fire crackle in the next room and the water softly splash. A young girl pushed past the curtain holding Charlotte's clothes, folded into a high stack. Before the curtain could fall back, he caught a glimpse of alabaster flesh sliding into the iron tub, the candlelight detailing the delicate curve of a hip melding smoothly into a lower back. Rone took a step closer and peered through the remaining crack in the drapes. He heard the clearing of a throat and found the young servant, still a few years away from maidenhood, standing idly next to him, doing her best to contain Charlotte's clothes in her arms.

"What do you want?" he grunted.

"Shall I launder the traveling clothes sir, or were you expecting to have your sister wear something else now that you've arrived?" The servant's face was clean, but her clothes were covered in soot and well-worn.

"Yes on both," Rone said, finding a polite tone. He pulled a small satchel from his bag, tied in twine "Do be a dear and lay this out for the lady." He placed a stack of copper coins on the cloth satchel as he handed it to the girl. Her eyes widened at the stack of money.

"Of course, sir. Would you like to wait in the dining hall? It will take us a few minutes to draw and heat a fresh bath after the lady is done."

"No, I prefer to wait here. And don't worry about the fresh bath."

"It was her request sir, and I don't much care to return tips."

Rone grunted. He watched her walk away, then carefully moved up to the slit in the curtain again. He could see Charlotte's shoulders and back as she worked a sponge over her skin. *Of course she faces away,* he thought. He clenched his fists a few times and sat down.

The servant girl returned a few minutes later and once again disappeared behind the curtain. This time as it was pulled back Charlotte turned about in the tub. Rone looked in compulsively and caught a flash of a breast as she leaned on the side. His gaze lingered for a long moment before he saw a pair of blue eyes, burning bright despite the dim light, looking right at him. Feeling a sudden surge of embarrassment, Rone turned his eyes away, to a dusty table near the kitchen. He felt suddenly hot and wiped a bead of sweat from his forehead. *You're better than this,* he thought. *Too long. Too much time away is all.* After another few minutes Rone could hear splashing once again, and a few whispers.

"Come in here a minute Rone," he heard Charlotte say on the other side of the curtain.

"She's not decent sir," the girl said.

"Don't listen to her!" Charlotte shouted back. Rone stood up and reached for the curtain, then stepped inside. Charlotte was standing next to the tub in a long white gown overlaid with a robe of deep red. Her damp hair was pinned back, revealing a clean white neck. She spun around, and the skirt lifted up revealing her calves and ankles.

"Looks good on you," Rone said, rubbing his beard. He eyed the servant as she pulled out the stopper in the tub, letting the water flow into a closed sewer beneath the inn.

"I thought you threw away all my things," Charlotte said.

Rone frowned and shook his head slightly. He watched the servant walk back out of the tiled bathroom as the water drained.

"Did I say something bad?" Charlotte said.

"I wouldn't worry too much about it," Rone said. "As to the gown… well, I thought it would fetch a penny or two if we needed, since it's silk, so I saved it. I didn't realize how well funded we actually were when I signed on."

Charlotte smiled. It was a slightly forced smile, and her eyes still seemed to carry the same sorrow as always. "Thanks all the same. My mother gave it to me. It was supposed to be a gift for my wedding night."

Rone raised an eyebrow as the servant came back in, unsure of what she had heard. "You're welcome, I suppose."

"Will you be attending to him, or will I?" the servant girl said. She reached into the tub and replaced the stopper, then added a log to the fire beneath the tub. She began to work the pump located beside the iron tub.

"I can attend to myself, thank you," Rone said.

"I'm used to it, if you're feeling embarrassed," the girl said. "Usually doesn't do much for me. 'Course most men who come in here are older and fat. Haven't had someone like you 'round here in a while."

"It's fine," Rone said. "I need no help. Why don't you show my sister back up to our room?"

"As you wish," the servant said. "But it's not hard to find any room upstairs. Shall I launder your gear as well?"

"Not necessary," Rone said. He cracked a smile at Charlotte. "Besides, I don't have anything pretty to wear."

"You're putting your clothes in the laundry," Charlotte said sternly. "I don't want to smell that old sweaty jacket even one more day."

Rone took a long, deep breath. "Fine." He looked at the servant. "I'll leave my clothes by the door. I have a spare set of trousers in my bag anyway."

Rone watched Charlotte and the servant pass through the curtain, then he quickly stripped. He hastily piled the clothes on a chair near the curtain, then stepped up and into the bathtub. As he eased himself down, he looked to the crack, half-expecting to see a blue eye staring back at him, but all he saw was the dancing firelight from the hall. He sighed and closed his eyes.

*

A knock sounded at the door, and Charlotte paused, her needle stopped halfway through a stitch in her torn cloak.

"It's me," Rone said, muffled by the heavy oak paneling.

"Come in."

Rone swung open the door, poked in his head and looked around the room, then stepped all the way in. He tossed his leather knapsack at the foot of the bed, framed in old carved wood that had shed most of its varnish through the passing of countless guests. He was wearing a faded set of trousers and a loose shirt that was once white. After he shut and barred the door, Charlotte continued pushing the needle through the tough wool of the cloak.

"We need to get you some more clothes," Charlotte said.

Rone shrugged. "Never cared to buy cloth except as necessary; cared even less when my daily attire was provided by the guard. Where's my pistol?"

"Your pistol? How would I know?"

Rone walked up and leaned over her. She shrank back slightly as he fished under the small occasional table she sat beside. He dropped a heavy flintlock pistol, with a brass receiver and an octagonal iron barrel on the table. He stood back.

"I want you to be armed at all times. This is especially important when I'm not here. You also need to keep the door locked." He took a deep breath. "I'm not trying to be unkind to you, and I'm sorry for chastising you earlier. I was not right expecting you to understand how to act. You lack the necessary experience."

"So kind of you to condescend to me," Charlotte said. She looked out the window.

"We will need to teach you some basic skills," Rone went on, ignoring Charlotte's reaction. "Do you know how to check the prime on a flintlock?"

"Of course I do. I didn't always live behind parapets."

"I assume they are illegal where you used to live," Rone said. Charlotte glared back at him. "Show me, then."

Charlotte tucked the needle under a loop of thread. She picked up the pistol and carefully lifted the frizzen. She shook the pistol slightly to see the priming charge move around in the pan. "It's primed. Are you satisfied?"

"What's the condition of the flint?"

"Plenty of life left."

Rone nodded. "Keep that one on your person if you can."

"Why did I hire you, exactly, if you expect me to do the shooting?"

"I expect trouble," Rone said. "I plan for it. I presume you care about getting off this rock, or you wouldn't have hired me, and so if it comes to trouble, I hope you will give it your best to carry on to that purpose."

"Very well," Charlotte said. She held up the pistol and looked it over in the lamplight.

*

"Rone," Charlotte whispered. She was leaning over the edge of the bed, the quilts wrapped around her. Her hair spilled out over the pillow and hung toward the floor, close to Rone's face. The window was still open, showing a waxing moon setting in the west, blurred by fog. "Are you awake?"

"Yes."

"I can't sleep," she said softly.

"Neither can I." He sighed and turned half away from her. "I never thought I'd miss packed earth, but these floorboards make me positively nostalgic for the road. What's bothering you?"

"I don't know. I keep thinking about... I keep thinking about going back. It makes me feel sick."

"Anxiety, then. Not surprising."

"You don't worry? They'll hang you, you know."

"There are worse fates."

"I know." Charlotte turned back onto the bed and faced the ceiling.

After a few moments, Rone said, "I don't intend for us to get caught, of course."

"I'm still afraid."

"Where's your pistol?"

"Under my pillow."

"Check the prime."

"I can't see."

"Just put your finger in the pan."

Charlotte slowly tilted back the hammer and lifted the frizzen on the pistol's lock. "It's primed."

"Anyone wants to take you, at least one of them will end up with a ball through their skull. Feel better?"

"A little, I suppose."

"Anytime you're anxious, feel for that pistol. It's a good piece and the barrel is clean. Only had it misfire a few times, and I've used it plenty."

"Thanks." Charlotte leaned back to the side of the bed. "What do you do when you're scared?"

"I'm not scared. Now get some sleep. I want to find us a ship out of here tomorrow. We're going to have a bit of walking to do."

"It's a big bed, you know, if the floor is hard."

"Go to sleep."

"We slept next to each other plenty of times in the highlands."

"We're not *in* the highlands, and it's not cold." Rone turned his shoulder even further away.

Silently, Charlotte turned back and stared at the empty, black ceiling.

IV: Three Sisters

harlotte dreamt. She knew it was a dream, like she often knew, but her dreams carried their own momentum that she was powerless to change. She was always a live witness, never fully lucid and in control.

She was in the Molney homestead, where she and Rone had stopped to wait out the illness that had struck her on the road. The ruined stone walls of the abandoned farmhouse were the same, but clean-cut rafters supported a well-tended thatch roof above. She was sweeping ashes out of the hearth, which was piled with the remnants of many fires, when she realized where she was. She turned as a little girl ran in through the front door.

"Mommy! Daddy caught a rabbit for us!" The little girl, wearing a simple duck dress, ran back out of the door. Charlotte paused a moment to look up, and a strand of dark, almost black hair fell in her face. She blew it away and wiped the ash from her hands on her apron. The girl appeared a moment later, then a man appeared in the doorway. It was clearly Rone, but he looked different. His clothes were of a strange sort, better made than what she was used to, and yet the garb was also simpler, lacking buttons and buckles. His hair and beard were longer, too, and his face was fuller, but his unmistakable eyes had the same glare as always. He stood behind the little girl with his musket and a freshly killed rabbit.

"When are we having dinner?" the little girl asked excitedly, clapping her hands together.

"We'll have to let your mother tend to the skinning and such," Rone said, smiling at the little girl. "I'm going to go chop some firewood so we can get cooking. You sure do like a bit of coney, don't you?"

"Of course!" the little girl said.

Rone put the dead rabbit down on the table and walked over to Charlotte. He kissed her on the cheek. "I'm sorry I haven't patched the roof yet." She looked up and saw the straw above letting in a few sunbeams in random places.

"It's alright," Charlotte said, "It's not going to rain tonight." She felt surprised as Rone pulled her into a deep kiss. His beard tickled her and she pulled away laughing.

Rone was gone.

The rabbit on the table seemed to look at her, though she knew it logically couldn't. Charlotte could hear the little girl singing outside, in a familiar tune, though it seemed to her like she had forgotten everything about it. She wished to run outside to the little girl, but couldn't stop staring at the rabbit. The words drifted inside to her, swift like a rhyme a child makes at play:

> *The point of a name*
> *Is that it's always the same*
> *Alone, or with fame*
> *Your name is the game*
> *With a name you'll see*
> *You're who you want to be*
>
> *And so the raven cawed*
> *And sat on his claws*
> *And asked what should I be called?*
>
> *I said 'you can choose*
> *To make your own news'*
> *He said "fine! My name is Zald!*

With great effort, Charlotte pulled her gaze away from the rabbit and saw that she wasn't in the farmhouse at all. Suddenly, she was back in her old apartment in Cataling Castle. Fine furniture sat against ancient stone walls. Her heart leapt, recalling somehow in her dream the horror of that room. Her small dining table was behind her, but she did not want to turn around to look, knowing the rabbit would be there. There was something unsettling about that rabbit, and the thought of it itched her in the back of her mind.

She ran to the door. It was locked tightly like always. She shook the handle. The hinges and bolts on the outside of the heavy oak door rattled.

She shook harder. Normally, the guards would notice her by now.

"Damnit!" Her voice cracked, though she tried to yell.

"Yes, mistress?" A voice from behind her said in a calm, soothing tone.

"Ardala?" Charlotte held her hands on the door for a long, drawn-out moment. "Is that you Ardala?"

"What can I get you? Fresh water? Are you ready for tea?"

"You survived? Rone said you had been killed for sure." Charlotte still could not will herself to turn around. "Why didn't you meet me at the wall?"

"You look tired. Shall I have the guards take you to the baths?"

"Why am I here?" Charlotte said. "I shouldn't be here. I left. I escaped!" She turned around suddenly to find the space where she expected to find Ardala to be empty. Feeling a sickness overtake her, her gaze slowly slid to the right, to the small table where she had eaten virtually all of her meals with Ardala, her only friend.

There was no rabbit. In its place was a baby, tiny and bloody, with unformed features; a miscarriage.

She screamed.

Over it she heard, as if near her left ear, a familiar voice. Serpentine and far too calm, it spoke old words:

*You are mine, child, whether you like it or not, though I suggest you learn to like it. While you attempt to regain my trust, I suggest you think on the poor women of the city. Who of them would not trade places with you, given the choice? You can cry if you wish, but know that **they** would not.*

*

"Begging your pardon!"

Charlotte bolted up. Her mind reeled. Quickly, but not quite instinctively, she reached under a pillow and found Rone's pistol. It felt slippery in her hands, and she realized that she was sweating. Her palms, neck, and shoulders felt suddenly cold with the moisture. Hands trembling, she drew back the hammer and pushed up the frizzen. A thin coat of powder sat in the pan.

"Relax, it's just the girl from last night," Rone said. He appeared from behind the privacy screen that hid the corner privy, looping a leather belt through his trousers.

"Your laundry's come back, sir! And madam!"

Rone raised his eyebrows at Charlotte as she held out the pistol uncertainly. "Do you think she's heavily armed? Or do you want to tell the girl to stand and deliver? I can follow your lead. Let me fetch a blade."

Charlotte looked around and took in the inn room, so much smaller than her old apartments had been. She was free, but not free. Safe, but not safe. She lowered the pistol. Rone gave her a smile and laughed deeply.

"You're a heap of nonsense," Charlotte said.

"My father always said that if you don't laugh, you'll cry." Rone walked to the door and unbolted it. Charlotte quickly hid the pistol back under the pillow and got out of bed. Rone opened the door and was surprised by a stack of folded clothes being thrust into his arms.

"Here's your laundry sir, hope it's to your liking," the servant girl said.

"As long as it doesn't smell like sweat and dust, I'll be happy," Rone said, dropping the clothes on a nearby chair. "Though come to think of it, just doing that would be a hell of a job. I sweat like a horse and smell twice as bad."

"It wasn't too bad," the girl said. "We have good soap, and my ma' was here to help last night."

"Poor thing," Charlotte said, stepping up to the door, her robe wrapped around her slender body. "You must not have slept at all."

"I sleep plenty, madam. Mostly in the afternoon. Quieter then."

"Still. Here's something for your troubles," Rone said, putting on a friendly smile. He thrust a large copper coin into the girl's hand. "My name is Munin." The girl looked up at him with a smile. "Now is why don't you tell me yours?"

"It isn't much of a proper name, but I'm Missy. It's all my pa' used to call me."

"Well I think it's a lovely name, Miss Missy. Now we know each other, and we can be friends, alright?"

"Okay, but I have to go now, lots more work to do before noon. Sir."

"I have a job for you, if you fancy earning a few more of those." Rone put his hand into his pocket and shook his hand, jingling coins there.

"Okay, but don't tell Mr. Sevelny. I don't wanna get in trouble for him thinking I ain't doing my work."

"I can keep a secret if you can. All I need you to do is listen. Listen when you come in and out of the common room, or when you walk by the master of the house doing business. You do that already, don't you?"

"A little, maybe."

"Good. Listen extra carefully today."

"What should I listen for?"

"Anyone looking for a couple of slave traders – a man and a woman – or someone asking about a female slave."

"I'll do my best." The girl looked puzzled. "Why would you be looking for a female slave? You're married, ain't ya?" Missy looked to Charlotte, who forced a smile.

Rone smiled warmly. "They're old acquaintances of ours. We're looking to run into them for business purposes, but I have a feeling some other friends of ours are looking for them too. Such is the nature of this trade. Nobody likes to do it in the light of day."

Missy nodded. "Sorry, didn't mean to pry."

"Don't trouble yourself. Just keep your ears open." He began to shut the door and stopped. "Of course, if anyone is looking for me in particular, you'll let me know, won't you?"

"Of course," Missy said. She smiled and hurried down the hall. Rone shut the door as he watched her go.

"Why did you give her that name?" Charlotte said. She stood behind him, her arms wrapped around her midsection. She was frowning.

"It was the name I gave at the gate. If someone picks up our trail from there, they'll be using the name of Munin."

"If someone is looking for us, won't the innkeeper just tell him everything?"

"I checked us in under the name Melanie."

"How do you keep track of all the names?"

Rone smiled. "You'll get used to it. We should get dressed. Lots of business to attend to today." He picked up the stack of clothes and frowned.

"Something wrong?" Charlotte said, pawing through the clothes while Rone still held them.

"These clothes are known."

***

Rone pulled at the top of his jacket, feeling constricted by its high collar and tight fit. It was a piece of style unique to Veraland, a doublet meant to look like a padded jack, but with colorful blue stripes stitched over the quilted linen and a row of buttons up the front. Rone knew from experience that whatever its looks, it was not a jack or a gambeson, and wouldn't stop so much as a pocketknife in a real fight. His pleated pants, baggy enough for him to keep his spare pistol concealed in the small of his back, waved in the stiff sea breeze.

"How is the straight jacket treating you?" he said quietly to Charlotte as they walked.

"I'll admit I had forgotten how uncomfortable a corset can be when it isn't properly made," she said back. She was wearing a modest blue dress, the skirts of which fell down in neat folds to the earth. The top had a built-in ribbed corset and bright white laces over gold ruffles trimmed her bust. She twirled a light blue paper parasol above her. "If you had let me buy the green one-"

"It was too expensive. We need to preserve our coin."

"You mean *my* coin."

Rone glared at her.

"I thought you wanted us to look like a rich married couple," Charlotte said, not turning away from the glare.

"I do. And we do."

"I look like a middle-class woman trying to sneak into a salon concert."

"All the better."

"And you look like a businessman nearing middle age, absconding with a poor woman that's much too young for him."

"That's what I am."

"We don't look like a young married couple."

"We're certainly starting to argue like we're married." Rone glanced behind them and caught sight of an old grizzled man flanked by two pike-wielding men. They wore hammered steel chest-plates, far from finely made or well-cared for, with leather bindings in various states of rot. Their green pants, however, pegged them as part of the town's guard.

"Always ready to dismiss me. If I-"

Rone gripped Charlotte's arm, silencing her. She instinctively tried to pull away. "Quiet now," he whispered, "It's the man from the gate, and he's got the guard with him."

Without breaking stride, Charlotte turned her head and glanced backward. "What's he doing down here?" she whispered.

"I doubt he's doing anything out of the ordinary," Rone said, and, tightening his grip on her arm, led her to the left side of the street. They could hear the uneven gate of the old man to their right and slightly behind them, as his hard-soled boots clacked loudly on the pavement. Underneath the rhythm of footfalls was the jingling armor worn by the guards. Ahead there was a break in the tightly packed buildings and the familiar triple steeple that indicated a cathedral dedicated to the Tranquil Sisters.

"You think he's the church type?" Charlotte said, nodding slightly toward the immense church building. Rone nodded back.

As the trio closed in behind them, they could make out bits of a conversation happening between the old man and one of the guards.

"I'm telling you, he cheats," the old man said.

"Yeah?" one of the guards said back. "How'd he do that, eh?"

"He keeps an ace up his sleeve, and the spade, no less," the old man said. "Just play a few hands and you'll notice. Only one ace of spades in the deck and he's always got it." The old man spat something onto the ground.

"The captain's sneaky, but he ain't into cheating with the men. You was probably just drunk," the other guard said. His voice was gravelly, speaking to a nightlife of more than just beer and cards.

"Of course I was drunk," the old man said. "It was Tuesday, after all." They all broke into a laugh. "But that don't mean I'm wrong. I can still shoot straight as an arrow when I'm drunk."

"No, you can't," the other guard said.

"Sure as snow in Materia," the old man snorted.

"Maybe we should put it to the test," the first guard said. "We'll stand up Colby with an apple on his head and you can shoot it off." They all laughed some more.

"A winning hand for the whole table," the second guard said.

The conversation was drowned out by the tolling of bells in the triple belfries of the cathedral, ringing in a trio of harmonious pitches that made a chord.

"Those are Notsra's bells," Charlotte said, not bothering to whisper under the din.

"Will that be an open service?" Rone asked. Charlotte nodded. He grabbed her hand and pulled her across a paved courtyard ringed with grass. They glanced back to see the trio of men pausing at the intersection. Their lips were moving, but nothing was audible above the tolling bells.

Rone dragged her past three immense statues on the outer edge of a circular courtyard, each facing toward a fountain at the center. As they walked into the center of the stone circle it seemed the marble sculptures, carved in the likeness of the goddesses usually referred to as the Tranquil Sisters, seemed posed to look down on them. Years of weather below an open sky had tarnished their virginal white, and everywhere they were streaked with grey. It gave them a life-like quality, adding to the three dimensions of stone a small piece of color. Each of the statues, though they were carved with delicate smiles, seemed to, with the grey streaks running down their faces, be crying.

Their walk slowed. Other people, young and old, ambled about the courtyard, all seeming to move steadily toward the entrance to the cathedral. Charlotte stopped in her tracks.

"What is it?" Rone said. He noticed Charlotte looking up at one of the statues. The sound of the bells began to fade.

"My parents always wanted me to be a disciple of Artifia," she said. The statue that held her gaze had long hair carved so that it hung about its shoulders, and in its arms, there was the likeness of a harp. "They thought I had such a lovely voice. It never got me out of cello lessons, though."

She turned to see Rone nodding. "You do have a good voice."

"I don't think you've ever heard me sing."

"Don't think so?" He smiled, though his eyes were sad. "All the same," he said. Rone's eyes narrowed as they focused past her, back toward the street where the three men still stood. She turned her head to look again and saw another man joining them who was taller and broader of stature. He wore something close to a uniform of blue and green, complete with an officer's jacket and chord and her heart leapt as she recognized the colors.

"Cataling," she said.

Rone swallowed. "They're probably in every port on the Isle." He looked back toward the church and nodded toward it.

"You recognize him, don't you? Did you know him when you were in the guard?"

"I can't see his face."

"If you didn't recognize him, you wouldn't be staring."

"Let's go," he said, pulling her toward the ancient house of worship.

The bells sounded one more chord.

She looked back up at the statue of Artifia, her tears falling upon her stone harp. Charlotte nodded at it and then walked with Rone toward the wide double doors of the cathedral. The faint sound of the three men laughing, a deeper voice adding to them, caught her ear amidst the fading bell tones.

*

The altar of the church, though gilded and carved of wood, appeared matched to the intricate stonework and flying buttresses of the exterior. It was three-sided and three-faced, with carvings of the Tranquil sisters immortalized in careful workings of gilded relief around the outside. Each goddess faced a different third of the round church. The artisans who created the cathedral centerpiece seemed to have been determined to eliminate any flat surface, and so the details of the holy place were lost in the almost organic lines of the whole. The stained glass that ran around the outside of the round cathedral was many-hued and depicted scenes from the Canon of the Divine, with one great window for each of the twelve gods. The mix of colors made the light around the curving pews seem hazy and dream-like, but somehow by the time it fell upon the altar it had become white, adding to the cleanly air of the place. Above those visages in a higher dome, three more windows loomed, greater than all the others, depicting each goddess arrayed in light and giving their gifts with bent knee. Upon the highest point in the altar stood a silver statue of Pastorus with animals around him in honor of his month.

The congregation was seated in the pews before the facing of Nostra, leaving the other two one-third divisions of the grand circle empty save for a few silent patrons in contemplation or study. The young faces arranged below Nostra's calming visage, facing the assemblage as if on display, wore a strange mixture of emotions. Some were painted with fear and anxiety, and others seemed to be disinterested, or even bored. The boys wore white trousers and the girls wore simple long dresses of green and white. Beside them stood a priestess, wearing robes of white trimmed with muted red and cinched around the waist with a red sash. One of the younger boys at the end of the row began to pick his nose, then quickly snapped his hand back to his waist as the priestess looked his way.

"And so, let us each give what the gods compel our hearts to give, for the maintenance of mankind, worked through the divine knowledge that shall be given unto these pledges," the priestess said. She began to walk down the narrow steps from the tranquiline altar, a narrow smile parting her smooth face. In each hand, she held a brass bucket, and when she reached the bottom, she handed one to the rows of people sitting on each side. "Some may become physicians," she said as she walked back up the steps. "Some may become nurses or herbalists, but all shall serve us as trade disciples these next four years."

"One of these girls could have been me," Charlotte whispered to Rone as they watched the offering bucket moved down one of the aisles. They sat in the last peopled row, and Rone frequently looked to the church entrance away on their left. "If my maidenhood had persisted but a little longer."

"Your parents would really demand you, *you*, ply a trade?" Rone whispered back

"They certainly liked to threaten it. I think it was mostly to inspire me to keep trim and proper, and stay out of the woods."

"For all the good it did you."

Charlotte pushed her chin down and cleared her throat as the gaze of the priestess fell upon them. Quietly, she reached into her velvet purse and produced a single silver coin.

"That's a week's worth of food, you know," Rone said quietly as the bucket approached.

"We have plenty more." She dropped it into the bucket, which she could see was filled almost entirely with rough copper pennies, the scraps that the poorest of peasants produced for change, along with the larger whole cyprals that were stamped by the crown. The priestess nodded to her as she saw the gift, then another cleric, a man dressed in simple black clothes, stepped from the back and picked up the bucket.

"I'm just looking the part," Charlotte whispered to Rone, who wore a frown. "Merchants are also generous."

"I don't know what merchants you've known."

"Well, their wives are."

"Which explains why the men can afford to do so little giving." He smiled slightly. The priestess moved to a lectern centered on the altar and opened a large book. She began reading from it, slowly and with dry intonation in the way only a cleric could manage.

"Do you think they're gone by now?" Charlotte whispered.

"We can stay here awhile longer," Rone said. "You never know. This might be an interesting tale."

"Unlikely, it's the fourth canon."

"I've sat through… perhaps three sermons in my entire life."

"Do you believe in the gods? In the canon?"

"Those are two separate things," Rone said.

"You can answer both," Charlotte said.

Rone smiled as he looked at the altar. "We believe in the gods, but not… Well, not as the gods they are presented to be. They aren't the creators, nor the guardians of man… or truth, even. They betrayed the dreamer and his eternal servants, long ago, and took upon themselves an identity which they themselves created – an identity which cut them off from their true power."

"I don't understand."

"It's hard to explain. The verse and the inverse, the mundane and the magical..." Rone looked at his left hand, frowning. "The canons bind people as they try to bind the world – to make it static. This place has beauty, but there is nothing here of eternity. Just the world that is."

"A true Somniatel," Charlotte whispered. She smiled as she said, "Not just a tamed barbarian."

"As heretical as you need. The Dreamer brokers no guilt for such things."

"Well, it's as good a place as any to take a nap." Charlotte coughed and pressed her hand to her chest as she noticed a pause in the droning cadence of words from the altar and noticed the old priestess looking down upon her again with a furrowed brow.

V: THE TRAIL

arthow handed the reins of his horse over to a stable boy and dismounted after he passed through the double-gated entryway to Masala Castle. Guards with familiar faces watched him from the house above. He caught the eye of one, a lad named Janry that he had put on a secret extra payroll to keep an eye on the guard for him, and nodded subtly. Quickly, he turned back toward the tall, wide stairs that led up to the keep doors.

The castle itself stood high above the port city of Masala, with a cliff to one side - an easily defensible fortress from a more chaotic time. Its foundations and much of its edifice were made of basalt quarried near the sea, and it appeared black beneath the grey sky. Holes in the clouds, moving swiftly toward the dry highlands to the west, cast strange shapes upon it that swirled and swayed. Flags flew proud upon the corners of its rounded towers, and the banners that hung from its front walls twisted in the crisp sea wind. Between the parapets, the shadows of soldiers moved slowly about.

As Farthow ascended the stair he heard a voice calling to him from behind. "Cap'n! Cap'n! Your woman's done sobered up!"

"Quiet, you fool!" Farthow said, turning to see Colby behind him, near one of the corners of the keep.

"Catannel's man is long gone," Colby said.

"I said quiet!" Farthow jumped the last two stairs and grabbed Colby's elbow. He dragged him toward the entrance to the outer halls. Colby shrugged off the grip and pumped his arms matching Farthow's stride. They passed through an opening in the outer walls and rushed across a dusty courtyard, their boots scraping over a floor that was as much weathered flagstones as dirt. An iron reinforced door stood ajar, a steel cuirassed guard standing beside it with a matchlock resting on his shoulder and a pike against the wall. He raised a hand to his head as Farthow passed by and nodded to Colby.

The pair descended a narrow stair, the wooden handrail worn smooth to an almost glass-like sheen. The door clanged shut above them, leaving them with only the lamplight below to guide them downward. The echoes of their footsteps shortened as they reached the bottom where the stairway opened into a low-ceilinged room, the floor made of stone. Years of dust had piled up in the corners. Another man, this one fat enough to look uncomfortable in his breastplate, stood near a gate of iron bars, chewing on something that was invisible behind his overgrown black mustache. He did not bother saluting as Farthow walked by, and Farthow did not seem to care.

They passed down a long corridor with cells branching off to each side. Some were enclosed by iron bars. Others bore banded heavy wooden doors. Another guard stood by one of these, twirling a set of keys on an iron ring. Farthow nodded to him and the guard unlocked the door. It swung outward with a slight squeak. Against the back wall, lit dimly by a small bared shaft leaning back to ground level, sat a young woman wrapped in a blanket. She was eating a bowl of soup with a wooden spoon, but dropped both when Farthow entered, pulling the blanket tighter around her and shrinking into the corner.

"Relax," Farthow said. The guard brought in a three-legged stool, and Farthow sat down on it a few steps away from the girl. Silence settled in, and Farthow smiled at her.

"I'm free," she said after a few moments.

"Doesn't look like it," Colby said with a sneering laugh.

Farthow held up his hand to silence Colby and said, "We're not returning you or taking you to market. I brought you here to help you sleep off the opium daze, and because I needed to talk to you."

"This is a prison, right?" the woman said.

"The best accommodations I could manage on short notice." Farthow pulled a silver coin from his pocket and tossed it to the feet of the girl. "Recognize that?"

Hesitantly, the girl picked it up and turned it over in her hand. "It looks like silver."

"The mark, you dummy," Colby said.

Farthow gave him a perturbed look and turned back to the girl. "Northmarch silver. A little odd for this part of the world. Where did you get coins like this?"

"I don't have any coins."

"But you did. Who gave them to you?"

"Nobody."

"There is no need to lie to me," Farthow said. "I promise, even if you do not tell me, I will not hurt you. I even have this-" He held his hand out and Colby placed a long box into it. Farthow flipped it open and removed a small pill of orange-black opium. He rolled it between his gloved fingers. "To ease the pain." He produced from the box a small opium pipe and tapped it into his palm.

The woman reached for it. Farthow quickly withdrew his hand. "Just tell me where you got the coin."

The woman drew her lips into a line. "A man and a woman. The man was tall. He had sort of yellow eyes. The woman had blue eyes. Red hair, maybe. She had it short, I think. They killed the man taking me to market."

"Were they his coins? The man taking you to market?" Farthow said.

"No. Not Marcos's. He was selling me because he was broke. He said he never would sell me, once."

"Opium?"

"Yes. Sometimes he let me have some."

"I see. What were their names? The man and the woman?"

"Munin and Daera. I don't remember which was which."

"Where were they from?"

"I don't know."

"Where were they going?"

"No idea. They turned me loose as soon as they got in the gate."

Farthow nodded. "Different business, then."

"How would I know?"

Farthow smiled. He handed the opium to the girl and laid the box and the pipe on the ground. The girl hurriedly picked it up and removed a small oil lamp from the box. Colby walked over and lit it with a match as Farthow stood up. The girl pushed the pill into the bowl of the pipe and leaned over the lamp, sighing as she drew in the narcotic vapor. Colby covered his mouth at the reek and stepped out of the cell.

"Let her leave when she wishes to," Farthow said to the guard. "But take her out through the south gate. And give her this." He handed a heavy linen bag to the guard.

"You're giving her silver?"

"It's not the coin she was given initially, but it's of equal weight. Somebody thought she should have it, so have it she shall."

"Suit yourself, sir," the guard said, and tucked the bag into his belt pouch.

"You're on your honor to do right."

"Aye, sir."

Farthow turned down the hall with Colby. "We've work to do."

"I'm thinking of the docks," Colby said.

"Me too."

*

Rone and Charlotte turned down a sloping paved street and the smell of the ocean began to fill their nostrils. The air had the dull stillness that characterized early afternoon near the ocean, when the winds began to turn from blowing out to sea to blowing back into shore.

"That smell has been a long time in the coming," Rone said. His feet fell hard against the uneven paving stones on the slope. As they turned a corner, an opening between two huddled buildings revealed a vast and imposing series of docks, freightways, and canals. Rone held her arm as they paused to look. "Impressive, eh?"

"It reminds me of the harbor in Fargana, only that city has a river running through it. As busy as a hill of ants."

They started down the hill. It descended quickly toward the flat walkway in front of the lattice of docks. The buildings around had grown larger and more packed together, composed more of warehouses, stockrooms, and workshops than houses. Between them and the ocean stood a forest of tall masts and rope riggings. Men jostled about in every free space on the old stone walkways, carting great boxes and barrels, and more than a few people in chains.

"Alright, that looks like it up ahead there," Rone pointed at an ancient sandstone building with a large front door facing off toward the harbor and surrounded by men. It was large enough to be a keep in its own right, though it lacked the usual defenses.

"My, it is big… Though I expected the silver seat of the west to have something a bit more…" Charlotte trailed off.

"Expensive looking?"

"Yes. Um... *current* is more the word I was looking for. This building looks a lot older than the castle, which is saying something."

"Aye, I've heard the keep has been standing in some sense since the fourth dominion and hasn't been changed for five hundred years." He stopped walking to turn and look up the hill, beyond the skyline of the twisted buildings of the city, at the massive castle that overlooked it. It appeared black at that moment, looming at the edge of a cliff over the sea. The clouds, blown swiftly over to the highlands by the winds above the marine layer, were casting frightening shadows across it that swam like a magic haze.

"If that's the case, it would have to have been built before the Harecs controlled the city," Charlotte said. "Perhaps the original keep for castle Hadelim?"

"Hadelim? Doesn't ring a bell. Hard to think of a time without a Harec ruling the Silver City."

"You know, the Harecs had an unenviable title in the south reaches of Latheria, once upon a time."

"Are there *any* titles that are unenviable?"

"Many, at least from a noble's perspective. The Harec estate was in a swamp."

Rone raised an eyebrow. "Still, I wouldn't mind the luxury."

"Somehow I think you, more than anyone I've known, *would* mind." She smiled at him. "You are much too restless to live the life of a noble." She sighed.

"You have me there," Rone said. "I had an opportunity for restful work, with the guard." He paused and looked at the sky for a moment. "Not meant to be."

"I'm sure it didn't pay as well as your current job."

Rone looked at her and shook his head. "It's not that. I haven't been paid yet, have I? No, there are some things you *have* to do. Things that are part of what you are, for better or worse."

There was a short silence where Charlotte stared at him contemplatively, then Rone said, "How did the Harecs end up here, do you know?"

"Vanilla."

"An herb?"

"It was, and is to some extent, the gold and silver of the lowlands. It grows well there. They made enough over the years to buy this fief when the old lords were swept away."

They were now standing a dozen feet from the front door of the trade offices of Masala, which stood ajar with a line of people reaching out one side. Occasionally a man in a uniformed blue set of trousers would walk in or out of the empty side of the door.

"I wonder what they did to be culled. The old lords."

"Some significant heresy, I'm sure," Charlotte wore a half-smile, and Rone watched the light from the pinholes in her parasol crawl across it. Her eyes, now a bright blue, glowed in the shade with reflections of himself standing in the bright sun. A strand of copper hair picked up in the wind and blew across her nose.

Rone stared at her for a long moment before realizing how close she was standing. He took a step toward the door. "How did you know their family's history?"

"The count of Masala was a prospective suitor. It was worth my time to know."

Rone nodded and chewed his lip. "Come on." Charlotte looped her arm into Rone's and they threaded themselves through the throng into the larger inner room.

The inside of the registrar was dim, but neatly kept. The thick walls and small windows were a relic of an older style of construction within the city, much more concerned with sturdiness than comfort. That concern was well preserved within the ancient docking agency, which (as Rone reckoned) held onto much of the contraband that was confiscated on site. On each deep-set window was a set of crossed bars planted firmly in the stone, reaffirming this purpose. The ceiling was stained a deep gray, nearly black, from years of candles, lamps, and other light sources. On one side was a set of tables with a stack of books and papers piled up on it. The line of people from the outside led up to it, and a mousy clerk sat behind it scribbling onto a ledger with a ragged goose-feather pen. Rone and Charlotte could hear him conversing with the man in the front of the line as they walked by.

"Fifteen men, twelve women, three child, just like it say." The old man was holding out a dirty sheet of paper that the clerk was eyeing over.

"I assume you will be housing them on ship until tomorrow?" The clerk never looked the old man in the eye, instead focusing on the scratchy writing of his pen.

"Yar, that's the plan."

The clerk handed him a piece of paper. "Take this to the cashier next door, he'll give you a set of stamps once you pay the total due. Be mindful of them, we can't replace lost stamps, and you'll have to pay the tax twice if your slaves pull theirs off before the auction. Next." Another man with a stack of papers stood up to the table. The little man didn't seem to notice Rone and Charlotte as they walked leisurely into the next room.

The next room was darker than the first. The rear wall contained a pair of great iron doors, double-barred both inside (so Rone assumed) and out, with two padlocks. To its left was a cashier's cage, iron-shod, with an old bespectacled man writing in his ledger beside stacks of silver and gold coins just out of arm's reach. The old man from the previous room walked up to the cage and, despite his ragged exterior, produced a dirty leath-er purse from his pocket and began to count gold coins out on the counter while the cashier inside began stamping a set of small papers.

Charlotte pulled Rone inside an adjoining room, suddenly bright compared to the darkness of the vault antechamber, containing the makings of a small office. A young mustached man sat behind a desk in the middle of the room, looking at a stack of papers in front of him and carefully writing in a large leather tome to his left. His uniform consisted of more than the blue trousers of the guard; he had a pressed blue waistcoat with brass buttons and a matching wide-brimmed hat, topped with a white plume, which sat next to him on the desk.

"Pardon me," Charlotte said sweetly. The young man looked up at her and smiled, revealing a row of white teeth.

"How do you do, madam?" He began to stand, "and sir," he said nodding to Rone.

"Well enough for the winds," Rone said, smiling.

"Oh, we're quite well. Am I to understand you're the dock master?" Charlotte said, tilting her head to the side.

"Not quite, madam. That would be Mr. Draggle. He doesn't spend time in the office. Too much paper and not enough salt for him. He'll be out making his rounds, getting ready for the wave of ships that will come in closer to sunset. I'm the count's clerk for the seaward offices. Lieutenant Dartan Corving, at your service." He clicked the heels of his well-oiled shoes.

"I'm Phillip, and this is Halbara," Rone said naturally. A slight pause filled the air.

"Melanie," Charlotte said. Rone eyed her, frowning in disapproval for an instant. Before he could fill the silence, she added, "of the wetland Melanies. Are you of the Southerland Corvings?"

"Yes, actually. My father's estate overlooks the woods there. My wife is from here in Masala. After her brother died, gods take his soul, we moved so that she could assist her father in his import business. The good Count Harec was kind enough to accept my commission."

"I'm sure the count is happy to have someone with such a good reputation representing his interests in the sea trade," Charlotte said.

There was an awkward silence, where Charlotte tried not to let her smile fade.

"Do you need the dock master?" Dartan said. "I don't expect him in until night."

"I'm sure *you* could help us." Charlotte smiled sweetly.

"Yes, my wife and I have a need to cut our tour short, and we need passage to the Northmarch," Rone said. "Bergen, Fargana... a lesser port would do as well. We will need to travel inland."

"Let me check," Dartan said as he sat down and looked in his great book. "Let's see, port of call Fargana... not its next stop. Hmn. Well, there is a ship leaving for Golice, but it's not listed as a passenger carrier. Brought in... dry goods. Spices." He looked up at the couple. "It might not be comfortable, but it's the only thing here leaving to the Northmarch in the next week. You can ask the captain yourself about booking passage, see if he's willing."

"Thank you, sir," Rone said clicking his heels, "How shall we find him?"

"He's likely on ship. Dock seven-B. Name is..." He checked his book again, "Johnny. Odd. Only one name listed."

VI: JUST JOHNNY

everal gaunt-looking men were stacking wooden boxes into hand wagons on the dock as Charlotte and Rone walked up to the ship. They stepped back as a young man staggered down the plank with another box.

"Who's this?" A young shirtless man wearing faded pantaloons walked up to the pair from behind a stack of boxes on the dock.

"How do you do? My name is Phillip, and this is my wife, Halbara," Rone said.

The young man stared at them and spat into the water. "You two don't look like our usual business." His jaw moved widely back and forth, working at a piece of chewing tobacco. His gaunt cheeks seemed to accentuate the motion, hiding no detail behind his thin beard.

"Are you the captain?" Charlotte asked.

"Naw. I'm Danny. First mate. Johnny's up in his quarters."

"Thanks," Rone said, pulling Charlotte a few steps onto the plank.

"What's all this about?" Danny said.

"We need passage to the Northmarch. Post haste." Charlotte heard Rone grumble beside her.

"This ain't your kind of ship, mate. Better off waiting for a state liner or something under a corporate banner."

"Normally we would, but I'm afraid time is a bit short for us," Charlotte replied.

"Suit yourselves, but don't say I didn't warn ya."

*

The Captain's quarters were dusty and dim. When Rone and Charlotte stepped inside they saw a large spectacled man sitting at a small table writing in a small book with a very ragged black pen. He towered above the back of his small chair, making him look almost comically tall. His barrel chest was pushed up against the table, leaving a fatty bulge pushing against the bottom of his tome. His jacket was hanging off the back of his chair, and his shirt was a faded grey, though Charlotte thought that it might have at one point been white. He stroked his long, black beard as he wrote. When they closed the door, he looked up at them and took off his glasses.

"What are you doing on my ship?"

Rone saw him reach down and touch a pistol in his belt. Rone felt his fingers reached for the familiar wooden stock of his own, hidden away in the back of his pants.

"We're interested in booking passage. We understand that you are going to the Northmarch," Rone said, doing his best to sound calm and polite.

"Golice, yeah," the man said, relaxing and putting his pen back into its stand, the end covered in viscous black ink. "But we don't carry people, unless you're part of the crew."

"We know there won't be much in the way of accommodations, and we're fine with that," Rone said. "We're travelers and we just need to get home quickly."

"Sorry, but I'm not in the business of travelers. Find a corporate liner, or a fleet ship." The big man put his glasses back on. Rone tossed a heavy leather sack on the table in front of him. He stopped writing once again and picked up the bag, weighing it. He looked cautiously at Rone and turned the bag out on the table. Silver and gold coins came out clinking into a small pile.

"That, and as much again," Rone said.

"So, you want to buy the ship?"

"No, we just need to get to the Northmarch." Rone said.

The captain held up one of the gold coins and looked at it closely with his spectacles, his mouth twitching as he seemed to consider it. "I still wouldn't advise it. When I say we're not in the business of hauling people, I mean it. It's really not something we should do."

"You're a pirate then?" Rone said.

"Privateer," The large man said, touching his nose. "Business is not exactly safe for ourselves; there's no way I could guarantee the safety of a gentleman or a lady."

"I make my own safety, captain," Rone said.

The captain sighed and put the coin back on the stack. "Well the sea may take ya, but I'll be damned if I don't understand risk and reward, and I'll be damned again if I don't turn away good coin. We're leaving at dawn tomorrow, provided we can get stock for our next shipment." He stood up, standing almost a half a head above Rone, and extended his hand.

"Phillip." They shook hands. The man's hand matched his stature: an immense paw that seemed to suffocate Rone's in its grip.

"They call me Big Johnny, for obvious reasons. I'm captain and majority shareholder in the good ship Parkitees." He looked to Charlotte.

"Sha-Halbara." She said, quickly correcting herself. She extended her hand. Johnny looked at her for a moment puzzled then shook her hand, taking the tips of her fingers between his own great thumb and index in an awkwardly dainty exchange.

He looked back to Rone. "Beggin' your pardon, Mister, uh..."

"Melanie, of the wetland Ravens," Charlotte cut in robotically. This time Rone softly groaned. Johnny's glasses slid down his nose as he stared at her.

"I meant *his* name," Johnny said flatly. He nodded at Rone.

"We're married," she replied. She hugged Rone's arm.

"You can't bullshit a man like me. You ain't married; least not yet. If you're eloping or whatever…" He rubbed the back of his neck. "I guess it ain't none of my business, but you can't fool an old liar like me-self. But don't worry. I can keep a secret." His half-frown turned into a wide smile, showing several gold-capped teeth.

"Thanks, we'll see to the other half of payment once we arrive," Rone said politely, dropping his air. He quickly scooped the coins into the leather satchel and turned to walk out.

"Dawn," Johnny said. His face relaxed into a flat stare. "We're not the kind to wait around. On your way out, tell Danny to set up a few bunks for ya in the high room." He smiled suddenly again, a strange glint in his eye.

"Alright," Rone said hesitantly, then opened the door for Charlotte. He raised his eyebrows at her as they exited. "Interesting fellow," he said after they stepped back out onto deck and closed the door.

The main deck, which ran over twenty paces between the captain's quarters at the rear and forecastle near the bow with a large central mast, was vacant save for a pair of deckhands busying themselves with loading supplies. Rone looked about for a few moments. The slim young man they had spoken to on the way up seemed missing on the deck and the dock.

"Excuse me," Charlotte said to a nearby sailor, busy coiling sets of ropes as he pulled them down off the naked yards. He was a tall man with messy blonde hair, wearing a shirt and pants of a faded grey, stiff and wrinkled from days at sea. "Have you seen Danny?"

The deckhand looked up from what he was doing, panting slightly from the work with the heavy rope. Though he was dirty and wet with sweat, his face was shaved and revealed a youthful handsomeness. "He sauntered off to somewhere or another in town."

"Oh-" Charlotte said.

"Just like him, too," the sailor went on, "to leave before even half the work is done. I'll probably have to do that poor sod's job, too. Be lucky to fetch myself half a pint before the night is through."

"Well, the captain wished for him to set us up a few bunks for us in the…" Charlotte thought to herself a moment. "Um, high room?"

The sailor chuckled. "Danny's not going to be too pleased with that task."

"Why is that?"

"That's the first mate's quarters." The sailor nodded toward the forecastle, which had a small door set a few steps down sunken into it. "The funny thing is, he hasn't ever slept in them since Johnny gave him the title. He's starting to think it's some kind of joke."

"Why is that?" Rone said.

The deckhand looked away for a moment in thought. "We had to use it as extra cargo space, then haul some kind of bigtime navy fellow from Golice, then we had this shipment of rare plants that had to receive exactly eight hours of sunlight a day then be put away. I think he was particularly perturbed about those."

"I suppose we could always bump elbows with the crew," Rone said. He coughed as Charlotte elbowed him in the ribs, smiling widely the whole time. "I mean… give him our sincere apologies."

The sailor laughed again. "I will. My name's Pierce, by the way." He put his hand out casually, and Rone shook it.

*

Charlotte and Rone paused for tea and wine at a shop around sunset, enjoying a bite of fresh bread and jam and relaxing midway through the long walk back to the inn. The wind coming off the ocean dried the sweat they had worked up climbing the steep slope back to the high part of town, and though they were well-dressed their hair had the crispy look of sailors. When they finally reached the inn in it was after dark.

"I'm about ready to fall into bed; the second half of that walk just went on and on," Charlotte said as they walked up the stairs toward their room. The fire in the main room down below lit the corridor dimly.

"Aye, that's the problem with walking downhill. Eventually, you have to go back *up*hill," Rone said cheerfully. "Still, the Highlands have made a climber out of you, despite yourself."

"Despite myself, what is that supposed to mean?"

"Prim, proper, polite, and protected."

"Not me!" Charlotte said through a wide grin. "I can't get you... you won't put two words together in one minute, and later you spit out the most scrumptious alliterations." Charlotte hugged his arm as he began fumbling for the big brass door key. "Prim, proper, polite, protected. You forgot politically passionate and positively pedantic. Or-"

Rone stopped her with a sudden rigidity in his touch and posture. While Charlotte was talking Rone had noticed the little girl Missy exiting a room, holding a small oil lamp. He had locked glances with her for a protracted moment before she turned away from his gaze and galloped down the stair at the other end of the hallway. The gaze had spoken volumes to the man, and though he knew he was out of his element in the city, he was not so far removed from his past experience to mistake the look on the girl's face for anything but fear and guilt.

"Yes, sometimes I fancy a bit of poetry, even if only to please myself." Rone's voice sounded cheerful, but his face was grave as he looked into Charlotte's eyes. He pressed his ear to the door for a moment and put a finger to his lips. He nodded toward the stairwell. Charlotte nodded. Quietly, she lifted her skirt and tip-toed back to the stairs.

Rone reached into his jacket and drew forth an old friend. It clicked faintly as he drew back the hammer. He reached over the top of the lock with his index finger and lifted the frizzen, feeling for a full prime. He locked eyes with Charlotte again, then watched her disappear down the stairs.

With his left hand, he turned the key; His right held the pistol at eye level. "Aye, it will be good to get some shut-eye." He pushed the door open. As it swung ajar, Rone could see a silhouette in the moonlit window. He stepped in.

"Ah, mister-" The silhouette could not finish his greeting. Rone swung the door shut. At the same time it slammed into the door frame, the butt of Rone's pistol slammed into the teeth of a very large man standing beside it. By the time his girth hit the floor Rone was upon the silhouette at the window, his left hand now clutching his knife in an overhand grip.

"Is it Munin, or Phillip?" The voice croaked as the edge of the blade pushed against his jaw. The man below sat limp.

"Speak right and live. Speak foul, and you'll dine with Grim this very night."

"It seems the girl was right to trust you. You also do not have me at as much of a disadvantage as you think." Rone glanced down to see a pistol leveled at his belly. "It's a hair-trigger."

"I'm good at my business, as it seems you are." Rone held back some pressure on the edge of the knife. Without breaking his intense gaze on the man, he trained his pistol on the man who had hidden behind the door, now lying in a heap behind him. "So, who are you?"

"My name doesn't have much relevance-" Rone pushed the blade again hard on the man's skin. "But it's Farthow, if you must have it."

"Why are you here?"

"Business, like you gathered. I'm representing a very wealthy and important man."

"In regard to what, then?"

"The girl, of course."

"I turned her loose."

"Not that girl."

Rone raised an eyebrow.

"I would make it worth your while to turn her over to me. How does five-hundred Aurals sound?"

Five-hundred ounces of gold. The price made Rone pause. His heart, already beating hard, sped up. His back felt suddenly tight and painful, leaning up against the stranger. "You could hire an army to take her for that."

"Not a very good one. And the value is in the prize, not how many men I hire to acquire it. I'd just as soon pay one than pay a hundred."

Rone eased up on the knife, bringing the muzzle of his pistol to Farthow, who remained motionless as Rone backed up.

"Who are you working for?" Rone said.

"I can't tell you that, you know."

"It matters," Rone said.

"Does it? For five hundred Aurals it ought not to."

Rone Swallowed. "Catannel? Or Harec?"

Farthow shrugged. "I can tell you it isn't Vindrel."

"Doesn't mean much." Rone licked his lips. "Can you get me off the Isle?"

"You're rusty," Farthow said. "Being desperate to leave, even without your charge? Makes me want to cut the price."

"I try not to steal anything without a way to leave safely with it."

"Bad form with the girl, then."

Rone chewed his tongue. "You could say that."

Farthow smiled. "500 Aurals and I can arrange a trip to several ports. I'll have it sitting on a ship in a chest. You can count it; I'll take the girl."

Rone took a deep breath. "Is it Harec, or Catannel?"

Farthow's eyes stared back at him, cold.

"Tell me damnit!"

"You know I can't. Just you knowing my name is enough liability."

Rone's voice raised to a scream. "Tell me who you're working-"

The door swung open once again. Rone looked away for a moment to see the man who was crumpled on the floor standing above him, also in the process of turning to look at the door. He never saw what had entered. As the big man collapsed (once again, this time against the bedpost), a slender body with long hair flying around it replaced him, holding like a club what looked to be a table leg.

In a heartbeat he felt his pistol arm being pushed up and away and felt a strike to the side of his solar plexus, knocking the wind from him. Farthow was up and out of the chair, but before Rone could level his pistol Farthow had overturned the table and leapt at the window. The move shocked Rone and he, without realizing it, held his shot, but Farthow followed through with his move, landing on the windowsill and sliding over the roof toward the street. Rone moved over to the window and looked down to see a deserted night street.

"Bastard is good."

"What was all that?" Charlotte said, panting as she moved to join Rone at the window.

"You just *had* to give us a last name." Rone eased the hammer on his pistol down and tucked it into his belt. Charlotte was breathing hard, still holding out the table leg like a sword. "But thanks for the backup, I suppose," he added, chewing his cheek. "I knew he was up, by the way.

"Do you think-" Charlotte leaned the leg-club up against the bed and breathed deep, "it was the captain, Mister Johnny?"

"Could be, but… I doubt it. Probably Corving at the shipping office." He nodded toward the window. "This fellow gave me the name Munin, too."

"So, a follow up from the west gate, then?"

"Aye, that's what I would think. Of course, it could be someone who was waiting for us all along."

"What makes you say that?"

Rone hesitated and looked into Charlotte's eyes. He looked away with a sigh. "Five hundred Aurals was what he offered for me to turn you over to him."

"What? That's three times my dowry."

Rone raised an eyebrow at her. He moved over to the large collapsed man and checked him. He was still breathing. "Part of me wants to wait till this bloke comes to and ask him some questions, not friendly-like, but I think we'd best be on our way."

Charlotte stomped. "Drat that little Missy, I paid her to tell us about things like this."

"Well, I don't trust most folks further than I can throw a coin. These two probably threw a bigger coin. But still, she did warn us, even if she didn't mean to. You can read a lot in a look."

Charlotte nodded.

A thud and a series of shouts from the common room below snapped them both to attention. "I knew he wouldn't have come alone," Rone said.

VII: In a Pinch

harlotte followed Rone down the narrow flight of stairs. He had his backsword in his left hand, tip forward, and his pistol in his right. Charlotte held the long gun awkwardly; with their packs on, they barely fit through the stairwell, and that left no room for managing a musket. They stumbled into the kitchen to find two men wearing bright breastplates and wielding basket-hilted broadswords pushing through, with the inn-keeper's wife shouting in protest. Rone jumped the last steps and kicked a boot out as he landed. His feet connected with the shins of the first man, sending him backward and causing him to topple to the floor, which was already slick with spilled soup and food. With a hasty chop of his sword, Rone cut into the ankle of the other man, and he fell backward with a loud cry, hitting the stove and burning his forearm on a hot iron pan. With a cry, the man dropped his sword and clutched at his smoking shirt.

Charlotte charged past them, making for the door. Rone got up and stumbled on the wet floor, just managing to avoid a fall, then followed her out to the alley. Rone, smelling the acrid fuse of a matchlock musket, pulled Charlotte to the ground. They both flinched as musket fire erupted from one end of the Alley.

"Hold your fire, damn it!" A gruff voice shouted. A group of men began scrambling down the darkened corridor, drawing swords and crowding one another. Charlotte and Rone, lacking any other option, ran the opposite direction. They reached the end of the alleyway and were left with the choice of going several different ways. Rone pulled Charlotte to their right, pushing her ahead of himself.

"Hope this is the right way." Rone looked over his shoulder, but his view was restricted by his pack. He could hear the shuffling of boots echoing behind. He faced forward again only to find himself toppling over Charlotte. He rolled off of her and saw that she was pulling the leather cover off the musket and drawing back the hammer. Shadows gathered where the Alley opened up to the street.

Rone slipped his pack off his shoulders and faced the way they had come. Four men were approaching, two abreast and leaving hardly room for their elbows. The front two bore long halberds while the men behind bore swords. Rone fired his pistol, hitting one of the front two in the cheek, causing him to drop his halberd and reach for the wound. He was quickly trampled by his fellows, but one of them, realizing what had happened, stooped to help the injured man. In a smooth motion, Rone shoved the pistol into his belt and drew out a long bollock dagger for his off-hand from a sheath secreted beneath his dress jacket.

Rone beat away the blade end of a halberd with his sword. Kicking at the pole of the weapon, he stepped up and stabbed at the man's arms above his gauntlets with the point of his sword. The strike failed to do much of anything, but it did cause the man to shrink back and try to fall into his guard. Rone, being still close enough to slip past the guard, thrust his dagger down into man's thigh. It reluctantly bit through the quilting of the man's leggings and found a bit of flesh. The man flipped his pole weapon wildly in shock and Rone stepped nimbly back. Two men were up behind him, but were held back momentarily by the flipping of the blade of the halberd.

Behind him, Charlotte scrambled up to her knees and fired the musket. Smoke filled the small space, and a man cried somewhere beyond the screen. His vision blurred, Rone tucked his dagger under his forearm and pulled Charlotte to her feet by tucking his fist into her armpit. He pushed her forward through the smoke.

Three men stood at the end of the alley in the moonlight, two with pikes and one standing back with a loaded crossbow. None of them appeared injured. Rone cursed and pulled up short, feeling his feet slide under him as he tried to handle Charlotte without the use of either hand. At that moment a bolt erupted from the neck of one of the men, just above the stiff collar of his breastplate, spraying blood on the man beside him. Shocked, the soldier pawed at his gory face with a gauntleted hand, which did nothing for him. The crossbowman fired, but the bolt was far wide, clattering off the stone wall of one of the buildings after flying past Rone.

Rone slipped past Charlotte and rushed forward. The crossbowman dropped his weapon and reached for his sword. Before it could clear the scabbard, the man fell forward, his head lolling. A hooded man stood nearby, holding a long, leather-wrapped sap. Hesitating only a moment, Rone reached back for Charlotte and pulled her forward, slashing quickly at the hooded man, who leapt backward. He shouted in protest, but the words were lost in more musket fire and shouts as men spilled out into the streets on the other side of the inn. Instinctively, Rone pulled Charlotte down into a crouch as he sidestepped to their left, down a steep hill, realizing in a few tense steps that the bullet report was distant. The men were firing in the opposite direction.

The hill bottomed out into a dense marketplace, still busy after dark with people crowding watering holes and eateries. The sound of the shots had elicited a panic from those in the streets and alleys, and everywhere men and women were rushing inside as barkeeps and merchants pulled in wares and barred doors, motioning straggling patrons to hurry inside. Musicians, playing in the open air for the milling crowd, were begging for help in moving their drums and chairs. Rone sheathed his blades and lead Charlotte into the midst of the crowd.

"He's following," Charlotte said with a croak. Rone glanced back and saw the hooded man moving unhindered through the churning throng.

"I think it's the man from the room," Rone said. "Here." He pulled Charlotte hard to the left, into the middle of a crowd. "And slip the pack off." Rone put his pack down and took her musket, letting each one hang from his relaxed arms.

She followed his lead and unshouldered her pack, letting it hang in her hand from its top strap. She followed him into a deeper mass of people. Men's and women's voices filled the pressed space.

"It'll be the coca sellers on Shore Street fighting again for sure," a woman's voice said.

"Doubtful," a man said in reply. "Sounded like it was coming from outside. The sheriffs again, I'd wager."

"Just as bad," the woman said in reply.

Charlotte and Rone went along with the crowd into a quickly filling inn's common room. The barkeep was standing on the counter just inside the door, a short two-barreled flintlock in his hands, held off his shoulder but ready for action. He was, in odd contrast to his posture, smiling jovially.

"Half-priced drinks for the next keg!" he shouted. A roar from the room answered him as a boy pulled the door shut and barred it. The bartender tossed his gun to a portly woman near the kitchen entrance and hopped down.

"Not the reaction I expected," Charlotte said into Rone's ear.

Rone grunted in response, then said, "I see another dining room. Let's see if we can find a corner for a few minutes."

"Do you think we lost him?"

Rone shrugged and wiped sweat from his brow. "The door is barred. Not much else to do."

They went under a low arch into another room, darker and longer than the common room with a low ceiling of old bowing rafters. Benches and tables crowded the walls and round tables filled the middle of the long space. They found an empty stretch of bench near a far corner, far enough away from the fireplace to be drafty, and pulled themselves into it. Men and women sat scattered throughout the room, uncaring of the pair, their backpacks, or the long-barreled musket that Rone leaned up against the wall.

Very shortly after they sat down a young serving woman approached and said, "What can I whip up for you? It'll be a while before the guard clears up the fight."

"You think so?"

The woman smiled. "It was an hour last time. Was only one man they caught though. Strung up the poor sod the next day."

"You've seen this before?" Charlotte said. Rone silently glared at her.

"Ah, you usually spend time uptown, then?" the serving girl said. "We gotten a few gunfights lately." She stuck her thumb out over her shoulder. "Poppy says it's the slave trade. Bunch of fellows come in from Tyrant's Gallow with teeth. It'll all be cleared up soon."

"We don't stay out often," Rone said. "But I'm sure it will all be taken care of. And we'll have whatever the kitchen's putting on special." He pulled a silver coin from his purse and flicked it to the server.

"To drink?" The serving girl smiled and turned her head as a young man slid past, touching lightly the small of her back before crowding into a spot beside the fire. He met her glance and smile briefly before turning back to his friends.

"Ale. Two pints," Rone said, smirking. "From the cellar, please." The server shuffled away, and Rone turned his attention to Charlotte who was wringing her hands and hunching over the table.

"Are we just going to sit here?" she said.

"For the moment, yes," Rone said. He took a deep breath and rubbed his temples.

"Why?"

"Everyone else is sitting."

Charlotte narrowed her eyes at him.

Rone sighed. "We'll be able to slip out with the rest of the crowd. I hope, anyway."

"If the guard doesn't break down the door."

Rone nodded. "I'll come up with something. Till then try to look like we've been here all night." Rone glanced toward the common room as some musicians started up a dance to a loud cheer.

"Would it be too auspicious to reload?" Charlotte said, eyeing the musket.

Rone chuckled. "I don't know these people." After a pause, he shrugged and produced his pistol and powder horn. He brushed the bore and reloaded, primed his pan, then slid the pistol to Charlotte. Nobody did more than glance their way. "I'm going to track down this innkeeper and see if I can get us a room to at least change our clothes in."

*

Farthow pushed himself up against the edge of an old stone building and peered out. Behind him, Market Street had emptied, and he knew Vindrel would be leading his elite, along with the men the count had attached to him under the token supervision of Colby, down toward the normally packed entertainment center. The Old Keep way was filling now with civilian onlookers, wandering out of their boarding houses and apartments with lit lamps. They all seemed curious as to what the gunfire had been about, several minutes having now past from the shots and shouts. A few men that Farthow assumed were soldiers were milling about near the end of the street, but they were hard to make out in the partially obscured moonlight. The marine layer had swept inland and now blotted out the stars.

A slight movement to his right alerted Farthow. He saw a flash of hand signals from a man obscured beside a door landing.

Status.

Several men knew the highland hand signals Farthow had taught, but he knew only either Dem or Colby were out in the night and near at hand. Neither of them knew how to sign their name yet, so answering was a gamble. He had chosen to keep Colby out of the know for what he considered good reasons. Bringing the marksman in on things at this stage would be riskier than if Farthow had disclosed his plans from the outset.

"Nothing for it," he said quietly to himself.

He stepped out and signed, ***Status – safe. Target – hidden. Behind. Meet me at the far side.*** He pointed down the meandering avenue that was the cluster of inns around Market Street. A figure stepped out of the shadows holding a crossbow and jogged up the lane.

Dreamer, thanks for that, Farthow thought. It was Dem. He turned and ran back the other direction to meet him.

A few minutes later they were together outside a bar with its door tightly shut but the exterior lamp left lit. A boisterous sound came from within.

"Where's Gareth?" Dem asked.

"With Colby, I hope," Farthow said. "He took a blow to the head and I had to leave him behind. I think our mark is inside of Poppy's," Farthow said.

"You sure?"

"Not at all. You know where the larder door is?"

"Of course. I get out from time to time, you know."

"See if you can get in that way. There's a guardhouse a block up. I'm going to commandeer a horse and intercept Vindrel and Colby."

"What do you want me to do with her if I find her?"

"Take her back to your place."

"My house?"

"Yes. There's that alley with the sewer behind Sott's. Should take you east enough to hit the Long Circle."

Dem chewed his cheek. "Shit."

"That's generally what collects in sewers. What's your point?"

Dem shook his head and shouldered his crossbow. "I don't figure they'll listen to me, boss."

"Nonsense. You can be very persuasive if you're well-motivated. Just turn on that country charm, and they'll come around. I'm going to buy you some time and flush some people out. You'll be fine."

VIII: Streets of Silver

harlotte felt uneasy as the moments passed by and Rone had not returned. Compulsively, she put her hand into her bag and rummaged until she found the leather bag that was stuffed with her gold. An itch in her mind had made her believe that somehow, in the rush out the door of the inn, she had left it behind. There would be no getting off the Isle of Veraland without that long-hidden cache. She breathed with relief, feeling its immense weight.

Rone had proven his word to her with that bag of money, enough to buy himself whatever life he desired, though the test had been unexpected. A day out of Cataling, while still climbing into the dry highlands, he had discovered it while repacking their bags, convinced that she was struggling too much with the weight. He had nodded to her and told her to hold onto it until he earned it; Charlotte knew he could have quite simply killed her for the money and never bothered with her promise of payment by her uncle.

"Charlotte of the Plain, I presume?"

Charlotte flinched at the soft-spoken voice and looked up to see a plain-clothed man with a well-trimmed beard sitting down across from her. She reached for the pistol, folded in her lap amidst her skirts. Trying to calm herself, she eased back the hammer and pushed up the frizzen, feeling for the grit of the prime.

"My name is Dem. I am not here to return you to your husband, so please don't shoot me."

"You work with the other man, then?"

"I don't know who the other man is to you," Dem said, raising his eyebrows. "I'm just here to get you out of the cook pot, so to speak. Vindrel's company should be getting here soon, but I know of a few ways out of this particular social area."

"Those men weren't the count's?"

Dem looked at her and frowned. "It doesn't matter. We need to get you out of-" Dem flinched and cut off his words.

"You make interesting friends when I'm not looking," Rone said. He was standing behind Dem's chair, his pistol, mostly obscured by his open jacket, was pushed up against the man's neck.

Dem put his hands on the table. "I have a safe house for you, at least until you can get aboard a ship and get out of here." He turned his head to look at Rone. "You're running out of options, sir."

"You work for Harec as well?"

"I aim to keep you out of Vindrel's hands, and that should be enough."

"So that was him, and he knows we're here."

Charlotte looked at Dem. "How will you help us?"

"He won't," Rone said.

"I'll slip you out the back door and take you somewhere safe. There are a few ways to cut through to the Garden Wall that you likely don't know about."

"I have a room upstairs," Rone said. "We'll need to change our clothes."

"That can wait," Dem said. "It must wait, really." Rone stood still for an agonizing few moments. Dem turned to him and said, "I wish I could say it doesn't matter to me if you come or not, but my arse is on the line here too."

The crowd cheered as the musicians finished a song.

"Let's go," Charlotte said. "Sitting around is worse than running."

"Agreed," Rone said. He tucked the pistol back into his belt and picked up his bag. "Lead the way…" He held up his hands and raised his eyebrows questioningly.

"Dem." He gave Rone a disingenuous smile and stood up.

They followed the lanky man past the fireplace and around a corner to a small room with tables overflowing with foodstuffs. A short door stood at one end. Dem casually flipped it open and ducked in, lowering himself down a steep stair into darkness. Charlotte went next with the musket.

"I can't see anything," she said.

As Rone began to duck in, a sharp voice rang out.

"Hey! What are you doing in my larder?" It was the barkeep, and he came stomping up to Rone, picking up a small club from beside the entryway.

Without hesitation Rone kicked the man in the belly, doubling him over before he could wield his club. Rone then tipped over a table of vegetables onto the man and ducked into the cellar. A serving woman that was walking by cried out as she saw the scene and ran away. Voices in the common room answered her.

Before he shut the door Rone yelled at the barkeep, "Your kitchen is slow as shit. I ordered soup half an hour ago!" He slammed the door and looked for a latch. He found none, and so descended the stair with renewed haste. At the landing, a small stone-floored cellar spread out. A dim light cast by a small lamp illuminated the low-ceilinged room. Barrels and kegs leaned against one wall and bags of flour against another.

"That your idea of a joke?" Dem said.

"You bet," Rone said with a chuckle. "If you don't laugh, you'll cry."

Dem scoffed and moved toward the far end of the cellar. "At the very least you'll be remembered."

"And here I am usually trying to avoid that."

He stood on a barrel and pushed against the ceiling, revealing a trap door. Moonlight spilled onto the floor as Dem reached down and picked up a crossbow, then threw it up into the light. He pulled himself up and out of the cellar.

His hand stuck down. "Give me your bags."

Rone pulled his bag off and handed it to Dem, who lugged it out and set it on the street beside him. He followed with Charlotte's bag.

"The girl next," he said.

Rone ignored him. He handed his pistol to Charlotte, who, lacking anywhere else to stash it, stuffed it between her breasts. Rone then pulled himself up and out of the cellar. When he was clear, Charlotte came and stood on the keg, her arms uplifted, and Rone quickly grasped her elbows with two hands and lifted her up. Dem had already moved to the corner of the inn and was gazing away, reloading his crossbow. He looked back to Rone and held a finger to his lips, then motioned for them to come.

They both quickly shouldered their burdens and came forward. The sound of boots and voices tickled their ears as they passed out of the cover of the building. A quick glance down the side of the inn revealed men armed with long guns and pikes laying hands lightly on modestly clothed men and women as they exited a different tavern. Occupied as they were, they did not notice the trio as they slipped into another alley.

"Here," Dem said. He pointed to an opening in the alley that seemed to be beneath one of the buildings. Stairs, wet with condensation and slime, were going down into the dark.

Charlotte covered her mouth with her hand. Rone motioned her down, and she followed Dem. She had to keep her hand against the wall to keep from slipping, and she had to kick out with her feet on each step to stop herself from tripping on her skirts. At the bottom, Dem swung open a small iron gate, revealing a long open sewer that ran perpendicular to the alleyway before curving away some yards ahead. The entire thing sat some six feet below the level of the street, with small bridges and even entire buildings going overhead, blacking out sections of the path.

"Don't worry, we won't be down here long," Dem said. They followed him through a short, straight tunnel that ran under a building before revealing the moon and stars on the other side. Openings from the street cut into the walls here and there, with water and other refuse dripping from them. When they could, they walked along the dry edge, but in a few places, obstructions forced them to step quickly through a few patches of sewage. They passed two more stairs and walked along a long curve before Dem motioned them to step up and out by a short set of steps. When they reached the top of the stairs, they found themselves in an unfamiliar street, lit brightly by the silver moon that was now overhead. A long ivy-covered wall lined one side. The street was quiet, nearly soundless, and their footsteps echoed almost painfully.

"I hope you're up for a bit of a walk," Dem said. "My place is down this lane. Almost to the outer wall."

Dem turned away, and at that moment, Rone struck. He swiftly kicked at Dem's back leg, striking the back of the knee. Dem began to collapse, but even with his heavy pack, Rone was already moving to bind the man. He twisted Dem's arm, causing the crossbow to drop to the street. It released as it hit, sending a bolt flying against the ivy-covered wall with a dull thud. Rone's dagger was instantly in his right hand and against the small of Dem's back, his other arm wrapped about the man's neck.

"Stop!" Charlotte cried, fumbling the musket to the ground. "No, Rone!"

Rone did stop, but he did not remove the knife, which bit still slightly into Dem's jacket, tearing the cloth. Dem, still struggling against the hold, had his back arched and was kicking to stop himself from falling onto the blade.

"Why should I stop?" Rone's voice was cold and distant.

"He helped us."

"Only to help himself, or the count, who is his employer, I reckon. He killed for that employer little more than an hour ago, and he will kill me if he gets the chance. We have no friends here. You should know this."

"I don't care. Please."

Rone took a deep breath, but whatever thought he had brewing, whatever rebuttal he was stewing up, was lost as they heard the reverberating sound of hooves. He pulled away his dagger and struck Dem on the temple with the pommel. Dem collapsed with a groan.

"Quickly!" He grabbed Charlotte's hand and pulled her down the street. They ran with all the speed they could muster.

*

Farthow dropped off the horse and pulled Dem to a sitting position on the street. Dem was conscious, but swooning, and gripped his head with his hands.

"Are you alright man?! Open your eyes!" Farthow held up his oil lamp and saw swift blinking.

"Bastard."

Farthow smiled, then said, "Which way did they go?"

"East. Probably toward the harbor."

"Damn it."

"What's our status?"

"I caught up with Colby. They figured out independently that passage was booked on a cargo ship. Some freebooter from Golice."

"Shit."

"Yes, you reek of it."

"You and that woman's man joke at the wrong times," Dem said as he struggled to his feet.

"If you don't laugh, you'll cry."

"That's what he said."

"Sounds like a real arsehole."

Farthow led the man back to his horse. "Let's get you on and get you to a healer. A real one."

"You mean an apostate?"

"Of course. I don't want you dying of a skull bleed."

"Thoughtful, but what about our quarry?" Dem groaned as Farthow pushed him up into the saddle.

"I'll catch up to them. I think this fellow has been here before, so I have a few ideas about where to find him."

"What if you don't find him?"

"Then we'll be in a spot of trouble, won't we?" Farthow shrugged as he led the horse by the bridle, running alongside to get the beast into a slow trot. "Maybe we'll have to pluck the girl from Vindrel."

*

Charlotte dropped her bag and bent over, breathing heavily and waiting for the ache in her side to dull. They had slowed to a walk for what seemed like miles, but the escape had winded her thoroughly. She took a deep breath and caught herself nearly gagging from the smell of the sewage still clinging to the hem of her skirts. Rone, showing no signs of exertion from the flight, pounded on the heavy wooden door again.

"Damn it, Getty! I know you're in there!" he rasped. Even with the tone of a whisper, his voice carried in the empty courtyard.

A board slid back revealing a peephole. Dim light flickered in the room beyond. A small square mirror appeared, revealing deep-set dark eyes.

"I thought I was rid of you. My debt was paid with your slave."

"What slave?"

"Not too many around here know me as Getty."

Rone grumbled. "Well, you have the opportunity now to turn those tables."

The mirror shifted its angle. "Who's the girl?"

"Not important."

Charlotte looked up and met the eyes, which narrowed on her.

"So that's the rub." The mirror disappeared and the eyes themselves appeared. "I'll probably never get to collect on this debt, will I?"

Rone held his palms up in resignation.

They heard a scraping sound as the door was unbarred and opened, revealing a small room cluttered with books. A desk overflowing with papers sat against one wall, and a small passage opened into a sitting room with an iron stove. The eyes in the door belonged to a lanky older man, clean-shaven with grey hair tied back. He wore a light coat over pants, but was barefoot. He had a pistol in his right hand.

"What exactly do you need at this hour? I can't imagine it's another forgery."

"We just need to sit for a few hours. We'll be out of here before dawn."

The old man chewed his lip. "So, the guard might be busting down my door, is that it?"

"Hopefully not."

Getty sighed and walked to the sitting room. Rone put his pack down and nodded for Charlotte to follow. Getty sat down in one of four chairs. Beside it was a tall pile of books, with plenty of papers stacked between. A tea kettle sat on the stove, not yet whistling. Rone collapsed into one of the chairs and sighed.

Charlotte stood for a long moment, looking at the remaining chairs, then sat down carefully in one of them. She stared at Rone, her eyes trembling. She then buried her face in her hands and began to cry softly. Rone held out his hand to rub her back, but hesitated, let it hover for a moment, and withdrew it. She lifted her head up and wiped her tears, then fixed her face into a serious and relaxed stare.

Rone looked to Getty. "Sorry, things have been rough."

"I can tell. I have a fresh pot brewing here. You're welcome to the tea, but if you need rest, I have that extra bedroom up the stairs."

Rone shook his head. "I don't think I'll be sleeping tonight, but I'll gladly take some space to change clothes."

Getty nodded as the pot began to whistle. "That's a good idea. I didn't want to say anything, but you smell awful."

IX: A Breath

The bedroom was sparsely decorated, with an old mattress on a low cracked wooden frame next to an occasional table with a single small chair. Charlotte put her bag against the door after she closed it, then put the pistol on the table. She sat on the mattress, which creaked as it sagged under her weight, and clenched her fists in an effort to get her hands to stop shaking.

"Sorry I got rattled," she said, staring into her lap. "I knew this would be dangerous. I guess I just wasn't prepared for the violence."

"Don't be sorry. It's not something I would have you get used to." Rone sat down and began loosening his shoes, the fine leather caked with mud and other things Charlotte did not want to think about.

"Are *you* used to it?"

"I thought I was," Rone said. He cracked a smile as he pushed his shoes off. "Ah, much better." He rubbed his feet through his grey socks. "Pretty things are rarely comfortable, eh?"

Charlotte smiled. "You're wrong. The finest things always look the best *and* feel the best. Of course, *these* are not the finest things." She reached behind herself and pulled on the knot, hidden under a wide ribbon, that held the built-in corset of her dress. It refused to release.

Rone stood up and unbuttoned his doublet and took it off, revealing a sweat-soaked undershirt. He saw Charlotte struggling and walked over. He leaned past her and pulled apart the knot. She felt an immediate rush as the laces up her back released.

"Thank you," she said. She leaned down to remove her soft shoes, now soaked and torn in a few places. A dull ache in her ribs replaced the release of pressure.

Rone smiled and took his shirt off as he walked back to his pack. "My apologies, but we haven't the time or space for modesty," he said. He slid his pants off and opened his pack, rummaging for his heavier clothes. Charlotte paused and looked at him. She had peeked at him impulsively as he bathed the night prior at the inn, but she had not been able to see much while hiding behind the curtain. What she saw now disturbed her.

His body was pale, drawn in shades of white like hers, but everywhere she could see his skin was mottled with discolored scars of pink and purple. Whip marks crisscrossed his back, and the evidence of smaller wounds dotted his limbs. A single long cut ran along his ribs, old and faded. And yet beneath these scars his skin was taught on a sharp physique; layers of knotted muscles were built onto a frame that looked made to endure.

She tore her eyes from him and stood up. She loosened the laces that cinched her dress at the waist and pushed it down to the ground, taking her soiled underskirts with it. Her bare breasts felt suddenly tight as the night's sweat on them chilled in the open air. She stared at the crumpled dress below her slip for a long moment, then glanced back up at Rone. She locked onto his yellow-green eyes for a moment before he turned away and worked at lacing up his pants.

Charlotte felt herself immediately begin crying again, with a shuddering sob wracking her shoulders. She fell back down to the bed and buried her face. Rone turned about and walked to her.

"Are you alright?" He said, holding his hands out but hesitating to touch her.

"I'm sorry."

"For what?"

"I'm sorry... I'm sorry that I brought you into all this."

"I'm the one who brought you here. I'm the one who dragged you across the mountains, if you'll recall. I'm the one who brought you into the city."

"You know what I mean." She looked up at him with reddened eyes. "Ardala... and now you. You're going to be killed. I know it. I should have just stayed where I was."

"No. You cannot count willful choice on your own conscience. I agreed to take you back to your home. That's my will. My choice." He knelt in front of her and placed his hands lightly, almost cautiously, on her arm. "Ardala made her own choice. I at least have the excuse of money; she didn't. Don't take that away from her."

Charlotte laid her hands on either side of Rone's neck, staring into his eyes. He hesitated for a moment, then inched away. Charlotte leaned up as he moved and pulled his head down into a kiss. She felt his hand on her hip, his fingers pressing into her flesh slightly. She let go.

She waited, her breathing shallow, then Rone turned away, falling back on his haunches. He covered his face with his hands.

"Why?"

"Because," she said, feeling fresh tears in the corners of her eyes. "Because it's my choice. Because you'll in all probability be dead soon."

"Have more faith in me than that."

"Then because I wanted to kiss a man for once in my life of my own volition."

"You shouldn't have."

"I'm tired of you telling me that."

"I'm a professional," he said, standing up.

"It's just a job, then? Just money?"

Rone sighed and shook his head. "You wouldn't understand."

She hunched over and closed her eyes, crying silently again. Charlotte felt Rone's arms wrap around her and pull her up. She laid her head on his shoulder as he hugged her.

"You're going to survive. I'll make sure of it." He looked at her. "Alright?"

"I'm not alright. I'm not *going* to be alright."

"Then just be alive, Charlotte."

He stood up, letting her arms drag around his neck, and looked down on her. His face was hard, but around his eyes a softness lingered, a squint that held back more.

Rone stepped away and retrieved his pack. "We should get dressed. That ship will leave at dawn without us."

*

Rone stepped through the small kitchen into the sitting room and launched himself backward, flinging Charlotte to the ground behind him. Sitting in one of the chairs facing him, drinking a cup of tea, was the man from the inn.

Rone scrambled, dropping his bag and trying desperately to pull his pistol or his dagger and cursing himself for thinking he was safe. He found his pistol in his belt, but as he drew, the hand of Getty settled on his arms and chest.

"No need for that! Nobody is here to shoot!" he said. A gun barrel popped out from beside Rone's hip. Charlotte was kneeling, the long gun shouldered and aimed at Farthow.

Farthow held up his left hand in a gesture of surrender. "I'm here to help! I give you my word."

"I don't believe you," Rone said.

"I know you booked passage on a Golician ship bound for the Northmarch. The captain is a man named Johnny, an old freebooter, though he will certainly claim otherwise. That ship is leaving at dawn, yes?"

Rone frowned at him.

"Tell your girl to put her gun down, by the dreamer!" Getty said.

"Don't shoot unless you need to," Rone said, glancing down at Charlotte.

"Perhaps I should give myself a more proper introduction. I am Farthow Bitterwheat, of clan Bitterwheat in the Southern Greenbacks. I give you my word that I am not here to do harm to you, Rone Stonefield. I swear by the dreamer that I will help you, and the Lady Charlotte, escape from Sarthius Catannel, if I can."

"Any man can name a clan," Rone said.

"But can any man name you, I wonder? I can draw the runes for you, but that would still require trust. I am Somniatel. That should be enough for you to know my word is true." Farthow leaned forward. "Now, I have named what I know, which means others know it. One man in particular, Vindrel, who I think you are familiar with, probably also knows it."

"How are you going to help?" Charlotte said. She lowered her gun and worked herself back to standing.

"I have a few things in mind, but you must trust me," Farthow said. He stood up and put his tea down. He held his left hand forward, palm up. "The armed man is to be feared."

"But the open hand may still carry faith," Rone said, and completed the other half of the ritual, pushing the back of his left hand against Farthow's palm. "I will trust you today. May oblivion take you if you lie."

Farthow nodded. He looked to Charlotte. "Now that the unpleasantness is behind us, let us consider our predicament."

"You have another ship for us?" Rone asked.

Farthow shook his head. "My employer cannot afford to be that overt. I think if we can get you on your own ship and get it out to sea that would be best. There might be a corporate liner going someplace else tomorrow, but I have no idea without heading down to the docks myself, which of course I cannot do."

"You have anything in mind?" Rone said.

"It'll be trouble," Farthow said.

"No different than tonight, then," Charlotte said.

Farthow cocked an eye to Charlotte. "Rumor carries that you're from the deep country and used to shooting and hunting."

"I am," Charlotte said.

Farthow smiled. "Then perhaps I have a good rifle for you. Better than that old smoothbore. Should be handy."

"A rifle?" Charlotte said.

"It's a special type of gun, technically a piece of heresy of course, used a great deal by sharpshooters and the like." Farthow walked to the corner and produced a long gun with a heavy steel barrel. "This belongs to my best man, Dem, but I can buy him another." He handed it to Charlotte. "You'll need a different sort of ball, too. I have some."

Charlotte frowned as she looked the gun over. "You said it was forbidden; why is someone working for the count allowed to keep something like that? Wouldn't the count be angry with you?"

"Who said I worked for the count?" Farthow said, raising an eyebrow.

"Rone did," Charlotte said. "And it makes sense. He's the only person in Masala who would care about retarding the plans of Sarthius Catannel."

Farthow smiled and put his hands up in resignation.

"You didn't answer my question, by the way," Charlotte said. "Does your Count condone heresy?"

Farthow chuckled softly. "What if I told you we had more valuable things than guns at our disposal?

Rone looked down with a smile. "In the world of politics, faith is nothing. Power is what matters. Heresy can be powerful."

"When we can get away with it," Farthow said. He smiled. "Of course, I make sure we always get away with it. Now, you think you can handle that?"

Charlotte nodded.

He gave a sideways look to Rone. "What about you? I've heard you may have a few hidden talents."

"Many," Rone said, "but if you mean magic, I'm afraid I'm as dull as you are."

Farthow smiled. "The talent's dwindling just like our blood, but I'm not completely watered out." He winked.

X: GLAMOUR

he sea was on fire as the sun rose out of it, burning bright with hues of red and orange. A crewman wiped sweat out of his eyes and grumbled about the hard work of the rigging, while others busied themselves carrying crates and rolling barrels up the gangplank and onto the main deck. It was going to be a warm day. The yards were being rigged by a pair of men on the mainsail. The dingy canvas sails burned umber in the brightening sky, still furled and creaking in the morning wind. Two figures in leathers, one in a long coat and one in a cloak, walked up the gangplank to the main deck, side-stepping a few shirtless crewmen. One wore a hood, the other an oversized travel hat, flapping slightly in the wind.

"Good to see you again, Phillip. And looking right and proper this time, too. It even looks like you've traveled before!" Big Johnny walked up to the pair, sticking his pipe back into his teeth. Rone quickly stepped forward and extended a hand. Johnny reached past and slapped Rone hard on the back, causing him to cough.

"If you're not dressed for the road, you've got no business on it," Rone said, smiling from under his hat. He moved to the rail and looked out to sea.

"There are no roads where we're going, lad." Johnny leaned back against the carved rail and spat into the water. "All the same, I had a feeling a silky doublet wasn't really you. You get a sense about these things in my trade. Bright colors have a way of making men like me antsy." He narrowed his eyes.

Rone touched his nose and smiled slightly. "Brown is bright in a sea of color, captain."

"That it is." When the captain turned around, the wind coming off the land in the early sun blew the smoke from his pipe into his eyes, momentarily making him squint. He pulled his black hat lower. "You'll be happy to know we'll be leaving within the next quarter-hour, just as soon as we're done packing the fresh stores. Good, strong wind off the mainland should push us out to the northern current, and we should be into the Pelagian winds by tomorrow afternoon."

"Speed isn't too much of a worry for us. Well," Rone corrected himself, "I'd like to leave on time, but the length of the journey doesn't concern me all that much."

"It concerns me. I'm a merchant. I have ah..." The captain paused a moment and closed one eye, "deadlines to keep." Rone handed him a bag that jingled. Big Johnny immediately pocketed it.

A sailor, who Rone recognized as Pierce from the day before, walked up to the captain and handed over a leather-bound book opened to one of the middle pages. "Everything seems in order, sir. We'll be pulling up the fruit barrels shortly, and I took the liberty of acquiring several fresh barrels of water as well as more dry stock."

Without turning his head from the papers, Johnny shouted, "Quarter-hour me boys! When that sun hits the deck, I expect to be gone. Let's hope the full hold makes up for your empty pockets. Better hope none of you got the rot, because I don't pay sailors to sit sick in the cabin with fire piss!"

Some of the crew cheered and laughed, but most seemed to not even notice the captain's remark. A pack of six men stood idly by, talking to each other.

"Is venereal disease a problem with your crew?" Rone asked, laughing.

"It's a problem with every crew. Can't tell the boys where they should put their precious assets, even if some of them are a bit...rotten." He grinned down at Rone. "Thank the twelve I haven't had sick sailors spread it in the crew."

"I don't remember anyone telling me about all this when I was on a ship." Rone leaned over the rail with the captain.

"No wonder you make interesting small talk. You're a man of the sail then? No, wait, you were a company marine. You have the look of a fighter."

Rone nodded. "I wasn't a good one. Conscription has a way of taking the professional passion out of you."

"Who was it? If you don't mind me asking."

"South Sea Trading Company."

"Not even a proper warship. I'm sorry, mate."

"I'm alive. They aren't. That's enough for me."

The captain frowned with realization and looked about him at the still men on deck. "Why are you standing around?! Pull up them barrels; the wind ain't waiting for us, ya know!" The crew stood motionless; those that had been working now stopped as well to see the commotion.

"It's been a good eight years Johnny." Danny, the thin and gaunt young man from docks the day previous, now wearing a loose-fitting peasant shirt, stepped forward from a small idle crowd of men. In his hand was a pistol, aimed at Johnny. Johnny stood calmly, pursing his lips and rocking on his heels.

"Ah, Danny," Johnny said. "Put that pistol away. Your mum would squint a lemon if she were to see you trying to mutiny."

"This is serious, Johnny," Danny said. "I've stood by while you've led this crew into pointless danger for the last time. I'm doing what my father should have, and taking over controlling share of this enterprise. Be glad it's not at sea."

Johnny turned to Rone. "Sorry you didn't get to know Danny here as the ever-loyal and righteous first mate, making this betrayal all the more biting. Suffice to say," he turned back, looked Danny right in the eye, and said with a flat affect, "I'm shocked."

"You should know better than to transport fugitives."

Johnny laughed falsely. "An old conscript, is that what this is about? Or are you just sore that you have to sleep with the crew for a few more nights?"

"Try a royal kidnaper," a booming voice said. A tall and menacing man in a green jacket, with a black beard and long black hair, stepped forward to stand above them on the quarter-deck, next to the helm. In his hand was a full hilt broadsword and the other held pistol.

"Wish I could say it was good to see you again, Vindrel," Rone said.

"Every time I think it might be good to see you again, I only find you to have fallen further, Rone," the man up top said, his face expressionless.

"I've never cared what you thought of me," Rone called back.

"Royal kidnapping?" Johnny said to himself. The big man for the first time looked genuinely shocked, even scared. Footsteps thundered on the planks as pikemen and musketeers dressed in a uniform of bright green trousers and blue shirts below shining breastplates marched onto the boat from some hiding place on the docks. A few barrels fell from the plank into the water as the crew stepped back to let them pass.

"Perhaps you have not heard, Lady Charlotte," Vindrel began, sounding as cordial as he could while shouting over the sea and wind. "But the Lord King of the Isle, Eric Grasslund the twenty-third, has died, and Sarthius Catannel, your husband, the Count of Cataling, is set to succeed the throne." For a set of seconds that seemed to drag out, only the wind, whipping through the loosened sails, could be heard. "Turn the girl loose and I'll make sure you avoid the torture chamber." Vindrel pulled back the hammer on his pistol. His thick black beard obscured the features of his face, but beneath his hat, his eyes shone out as a green amber.

"A quick death then? I could just as easily have that right here." Rone looked up at Vindrel.

"Don't count on it," Vindrel said. "And it's better than you deserve."

"Why don't you just give me half your commission? That's a better bargain."

"Always joking at the wrong time. You could have had your own commission," Vindrel said, "You could have been a great spymaster – to a king, no less – but once again you are too proud to do anything on account of me."

"Well, without me you'd have no job to do out here, so I'd say I'm entitled to at least twenty percent."

"There's no bargaining your way out of this one. I have you, and the lady, whether you cooperate or not." Vindrel then called out louder, "My lady, please stop cowering behind this vagabond and come to safety. Your husband, the rightful king, is most worried for your safety."

One of the halberdiers on the deck walked toward the trio. He extended his hand toward the figure hiding behind Rone. There was a flash of movement, then he drew back a bloody stump, which he stared at in silence for a few moments before falling to his knees. As he kneeled on the deck he looked under the hood to see a pair of green eyes and a close-trimmed blonde beard that Johnny had missed and that none of the crew had thought twice about; in fact, virtually none of the crew up to that moment seemed to even remember that the figure had been standing on the deck, and those who did could have sworn that it was a small, feminine form, not a broad-shouldered man with a full beard.

"Glamour," Johnny breathed in disbelief, the lone sound that carried over the silence of the bloody moment.

It was Farthow. Crimson drops fell from the dagger in front of him.

The soldier screamed, as if suddenly realizing the horror of his injury.

Before he could react to the bloody spectacle of the shrieking, shocked soldier, Vindrel grunted at a sharp pain in the bottom of his ribs. In surprise, he pulled the trigger of his pistol. Smoke swirled as he shot, but he missed Rone wide, hitting the railing and sending wooden shards and splinters into the face of a nearby mutineer.

"They have cover from the docks!" One of the Cataling soldiers shouted. Several of the soldiers around him joined him in turning toward the docks, suddenly afraid of some hidden enemy in the jumble of tack stacked dockside.

Moments later, Farthow's hood was off and he was running through the deckhands that encircled them, slashing wildly with a broadsword and stabbing with a dagger, leaving arcs of blood where he had stood moments before. Rone at the same time ran forward, batting aside the ends of pikes with his backsword and slashing with his long dagger at wrists and necks. He put down two of the soldiers in front of him with his backsword, who swung their long battle pikes uselessly in the close quarters, before drawing his pistol and leveling it at Vindrel. Rone held the shot, watching the black-bearded man slowly slide down the wooden rail and collapse on the quarter deck near the wheel.

Johnny did not waste the moment of confusion, or spend time wondering over whatever spell Farthow had managed. He drew his cutlass and put it to work against two musketeers, who fired even as their blood splashed on the deck. Johnny was knocked down by a pikeman's knee strike before he could turn to face the men who closed from dockside. Muskets exploded all over the deck, filling the air with black smoke, but Rone and Farthow were already out of the way, hacking a path through the soldiers on either side. Those who still held their live muskets were afraid to fire on their comrades, instead trying to put to use their sidearms. Sailors who had held back from the mutiny, apparently not privy to Danny's plan, now busied themselves with the soldiers and the men surrounding Danny, fighting with blade or grappling as opportunity allowed. Some fought with what was handy – a stick here or a knife there, but already cutlasses were being pulled from the inside racks and put into ready hands.

Johnny, still floored, flinched at the shots and rolled on the deck, trying desperately to avoid the thrusts and slashes of the pikeman above him. He hit his head on the railing after rolling away from a near miss and found himself swooning. When a soldier finally readied himself for a killing blow, pulling his great spear far back past his shoulders, Johnny picked his knees up, reached into his pants, and fired a hidden pistol. The pikeman's breastplate sparked and then began dripping blood from a blackened circle under his ribs.

Within few minutes, though it felt far longer to those in the fight, the struggle on deck began to turn into a rout as mutineers and soldiers, filled with fear and unable to regroup, began to jump off the ship or back down the gangplank. Musketeers, now freed of the burden of friendly fire, unleashed a half-hearted and half-aimed volley up to the main deck, striking a single mutineer by chance but otherwise only pummeling the wood of the ship. Rone rushed forward after the volley and kicked at the gangplank. It wobbled and flexed but did not drop. A pikeman rushed up to stab him and Rone turned aside, then fired his pistol at the man. The shot hit the man high on the thigh, sending him limping backward minus his pike.

Farthow began throwing things at the retreating soldiers: small barrels, bottles, rocks, and chunks of wood – whatever was immediately handy. He knocked over one of the fruit barrels and Rone jumped over to help him push it down the gangplank. It bounced and bounded down, cracking the timber of the plank and knocking two stubborn pikemen into the bay. Three musketeers on the dock, who had failed to see the rout behind them, stopped and looked quickly at one another, their guns spent, then rushed away from the ship as Farthow continued throwing refuse.

Rone turned to look for Big Johnny. The captain stood holding a pistol to Danny, who in turn had a sword trained on him. The surrounding men had stopped to watch, and Rone could not tell who was loyal and who was a traitor.

"You know why I had to do it," Danny said. His eyes were hot with anger and fear.

"Aye, just business and all that. I don't think that'll keep you out of hell though." The captain looked to his left at the dock. "Still time to step off, my boy."

Danny shot forward with his left foot, his sword extending at what would have been a potent thrust, had the sword been a rapier and not a cutlass. Johnny, despite his size, stepped backward just as quickly, and the blow fell short. The hammer of Johnny's pistol snapped forward. The flint sparked and the pan flashed, but the gun failed to fire. Johnny held his arms out in a wide pose. "I guess you got me after all, Danny boy. Tell that pretty mum of yours I went out smiling." Danny drew back to strike the captain, and in turn Johnny, moving in a flash, drew a knife from the small of his back and rushed him.

He stopped short as a spray of blood erupted out of Danny's shoulder, blinding Johnny and causing him to stumble. He recovered quickly, faster than Danny. The big man gripped the first mate's right hand with his own free left, pushing the first mate's cutlass away harmlessly. Johnny drove his dagger home, punching it deep into Danny's chest.

The first mate's muscles went lax and he crumpled to the deck, his sword clanking against the hard oak as he reached for his chest, red death oozing between his fingers. He struggled for a few seconds, breath catching, eyes looking out to nothing, then he ceased to move. A few yards away, Rone and Farthow flinched. Farthow sheathed his blades, turned, and bowed toward the shore.

"Full of surprises," Rone said. He took a deep breath and looked to the rooftop of the closest dock house, where a small shadow stood up and disappeared, two long guns resting on its shoulder. Behind him, the mutineers that remained were holding their hands up, forced into a corner of the deck.

"You better get your lass quick, before the guard figures where the commotion's been. Don't think they'll let you get away just because those weren't Harec's men," Johnny said, cleaning the blood off of his face with a dirty cloth.

"She'll be here shortly," Rone said as he took the steps to the quarter deck.

When he arrived near the helm, what he saw was a desperate and fading Vindrel, a small pool of sticky blood beneath him. He was shoving a short ramrod into his pistol. Rone nimbly kicked the gun away and Vindrel rolled over and looked at him, gasping.

"Looks like you got me." Vindrel croaked. Rone nodded. "I knew you'd never have the balls to fight me square."

"Apparently not. Too bad I didn't get to see if you'd lost a step with your sword."

"Couldn't see if you had or not, being laid out up here, but I guess you've gained a step or two in tactics. Never would have thought with how bad you were at chess and poker"

"I do what I can." Rone kneeled beside Vindrel.

"I thought I had you."

"Every hand is a gamble, Vindy. We both know it."

"Still, this wouldn't be where I'd choose to end this game."

"The game was rigged from the start, I'm afraid," Rone said.

"Why did you take the job? If you only knew the risks-" Vindrel coughed hard again.

"I know the risks."

"Someone's gotta be making you a rich man. Who is it? Tell me before I go."

"I am a rich man. Right now, I'm wealthier than the King of the Isle. I hold his crown, for now."

"If you only knew what she really means… But who are you trading her too, eh? Datalia? Draesen Empire? I don't want to leave without knowing... it's silly, I know."

"You're a mercenary like me. In the end, we only work for ourselves."

"I'm a commissioned officer, Rone." Vindrel coughed.

"All the same."

"I couldn't ask you to do me the favor of giving me what I promised you..."

"You mean a swift death?"

Vindrel's eyes widened. "Aye."

"Sorry Vindy, I can't do that." Rone rolled Vindrel over and ripped the shirt from his back. Low on his ribs he could see the bullet wound, leaking slowly. Ignoring the painful cries from Vindrel, Rone pushed his two longest fingers in and withdrew a malformed slug. "You are a lucky man today. Your ribs stopped the slug dead." Rone pulled a wad of cloth from his pocket and shoved it into the open wound. "This will stop the bleeding till a proper surgeon can stitch you up. I'd say you have a better than even chance of living, but of course you know how bad I am at odds. This is going to hurt."

Rone picked up Vindrel and carried him on his shoulder to the gangplank, dropping him as gently as he could on the dock, which was strangely deserted after the fight. A hooded figure, wrapped in a cloak and worn clothes that revealed a feminine form, was jogging up to the boat with two muskets slung across her back. As she passed, Rone looked under her hood to see a strand of copper hair and a pair of bright blue eyes staring back at him. They trembled, reflecting the bright scene around them, and behind their familiar warmth, Rone detected a dissonance that was new and disconcerting. He felt a moment of remorse for a piece of beauty that he knew could no longer be preserved as it was.

"This isn't much like you, Rone," Vindrel croaked.

"What isn't?" Rone said, turning back to look on the wincing man who was trying to push himself back up on his elbows.

"You leaving a loose end. Why?"

"Things change. Or maybe they don't." He looked away with a sigh. "I've always left loose ends when it comes to you. Don't die, Vindy. I may never have much to wager on a game of poker with you, but I'll risk what I have if I see you again."

"Anchor's up! Let's get out of here!" Johnny's voice called out behind him. Rone could see a group of red and green-clad musketeers moving across the stone freight way toward the dock, walking slowly. With them were a few of the Cataling men, who seemed hesitant to hurry ahead.

"Time for me to go," Rone said. Vindrel looked back up at him, frowning, as if watching something terrible to bear.

"Rone…" he said, trailing off and reaching up to the empty air as Rone trotted up the gangplank. The ship began to move as the plank was hauled up behind him.

XI: CADENCE

The boat rocked slightly from aft to stern, causing hanging trinkets in the captain's cabin to jingle. The slanting sunlight cutting through the dingy windows shifted across the table Charlotte shared with Rone and Farthow, who held a whiskey-soaked rag to his bleeding neck. Charlotte felt slightly queasy. She rolled the rifle lightly in her hands, remembering the two men she had shot. Though distant, their faces seemed to return in her idle thoughts.

"Something bothering you?" Rone said.

"I don't know how I should feel," Charlotte said, breaking the silence.

"About shooting those men?" Rone said.

"Do you think he was a bad man?"

"The first mate?" Farthow said. "Mutiny is a death sentence at sea. I'd say you gave him as good as he deserved."

"What about the other one?" Charlotte said. She pulled her hand through her tangled hair absent-mindedly.

"Vindrel's no worse than I am, I suppose," Rone said.

"You know him?" Farthow said.

"You were a member of the guard with him, right?" Charlotte said. "You talked about him before."

Rone nodded. "I've known him a long time. He's a stubborn man. He'll live. What about you?" He craned his neck to look more squarely at Farthow.

"If I die it's going to be an awfully slow and pitiful death." Farthow smiled and turned the rag over to another clean spot. He put fresh whiskey on it and touched it to the wound, wincing slightly. "It's starting to clot up, though I do think I'll be wearing high-collared jackets for a while."

The door swung inward and Johnny swept in, wiping sweat from his face and grumbling. He saw Farthow dabbing at his wound and said, "You owe me twenty cyprals for the whiskey. It was quite the malt, I should tell you."

"I wouldn't know; cuts don't taste anything but burning," Farthow said.

"Not my fault you didn't bother to taste it before wasting it on a cut," Johnny said. He pulled from his desk a set of logs and rolled maps, and threw them on the table.

Farthow shrugged. "Best way I know of staving off blood poisoning." He looked sideways at Johnny. "You're in good spirits for a man who just suffered a mutiny," Farthow said.

"Not just that," Johnny said. "Danny was more than just my first mate. And now I have to bury him. It should never have been this way." His face darkened as he looked over Rone and Charlotte. "Looking death in the eyes and walking away from it has a way of inspiring a certain sardonic humor. Now," his eyes narrowed as he took his own chair at the table. "Just who in the High bloody House of the Divine are you?"

"We told you our names," Rone said.

"You lied," Johnny said.

"You said it was none of your business."

"That was before I had to kill or sack half my crew and become an outlaw in one of my favorite trade hubs."

"I can remedy that," Farthow said.

"I'd appreciate the gesture – that is, I *would* if I knew who the hell *you* were as well," Johnny said.

"Farthow Bitterwheat, spy, apostate, and waster of whiskey, at your service." He nodded his head.

Johnny produced a pipe then set about looking for a match in his pockets. "Things have gotten complicated, and I need to know who I'm taking on."

Charlotte straightened up. "I am Melanie Halbara. That is all you need to know."

"Is it?" Johnny said. "Yesterday your name was Halbara Melanie."

Charlotte felt herself begin to blush and raised her chin even higher. "I believe you misheard."

"Where are you from?"

"We are... from the lowlands."

Johnny found a match in one of his many pockets and began lighting the pipe. "Not with hair like that you're not. You're from the Northmarch or I'm a slug. And this sell-sword of yours is definitely highland stock. That fellow you shot was an officer from Cataling; pity I didn't catch what he called you." He let a large smoke ring fly, then leaned forward. "Let me say, Charlotte, that rumors of the beauty of the Lady of Winter fall short of reality."

"I don't know what you are talking about," Charlotte said. She looked to Rone to see wide eyes over a blank face.

"I told you that you can't lie to a liar." Johnny laughed and smoke escaped from his nostrils. "That painting of you in Maragard doesn't do you justice." He raised an eyebrow to Rone.

Rone raised his chin and sucked in his cheeks. "My name is Rone. That should suffice for you."

Johnny grumbled and chuckled at the same time. "And I always tell people Johnny is enough to shake on. Fair enough." He spread out one of the maps. "My next question is to why we have no pursuit. Sailing off seems a bit too easy. You have something in store for me?" He laid a closed inkwell on a corner of the map to hold it down.

"Usually if something is too easy somebody has their hand in it. In this case, it was Drath Harec, who will be very grateful for your involvement, Mister..." He raised his eyebrows expectantly.

"Just Johnny, like I said." He drew on the pipe again. "Why?"

Farthow shrugged. He looked at Rone for a moment, smiled and said, "Why not?" He looked at Johnny. "Although distantly related to Count Catannel, Drath is still in succession for the throne in an eventual sort of way, and the ancient code of the Isle holds that in order for a king to be crowned there must be a queen to crown as well. Political opportunity abounds when there's no monarch to be found. There's more to it than that, of course, but I can't tell you most of it."

"Ah, the spiders of nobility, in whose twisted webs we common folk are but flies," Johnny said.

Farthow looked to Charlotte. "I had also promised to help you leave here in one piece. We had originally intended to take over your ladyship's chaperone position." Farthow bowed his head. "But not with intent to harm you, of course. If only you had gone to Dem's house..." He smiled and shook his head. "Drath will make a good show of trying to apprehend the kidnappers, but it will seem that the bandits had a ship that could mysteriously sail against the wind. Perhaps some work of sorcery. The story will tell that even the Count's best interceptors had to sail far out to sea before they were able to turn north, and unfortunately, the ship was nowhere to be found – vanished."

"So now I'll be labeled a heretic *and* an outlaw."

"You *aren't* an outlaw?" Rone said. Johnny narrowed his eyes.

"I wouldn't worry about it," Farthow said with a smile. "The dockmaster is not a fastidious record keeper, as I'm sure we shall soon find out."

Johnny looked over the map, which showed most of the North Pelagian between Veraland and the High Isles, with the divine strand, the Petty Kingdoms, and the greater parts of the mainland missing from the bottom of the chart. He pointed at an island near the southern end of a great archipelago. He glanced at Farthow "Now I'm carrying an extra man, and not the sort I like. Can you find your way from Nantien?"

"I thought we were going to Golice?" Charlotte said. She stood up straighter.

"That was before half my crew got slaughtered or run overboard," Johnny said.

"Upset that we saved your skin?" Farthow said.

"It was you that put it on the boil, you bastard," Johnny said. "But either way I'll have to dock before Golice to hire more crew. Calling what I've got a skeleton is giving too much credit to the crew and too little to bones. I also know a goodly portion of our stores were left on the docks. There'll be no room on this ship for idle hands the next few days."

"In that case, I think I can depart a bit sooner than Nantien," Farthow said. "We're not out to the open sea just yet, are we?"

"No, I was counting on the line ships being unable to rig effectively against this crosswind."

"Good," Farthow said with a smile.

"What do you mean by idle hands?" Charlotte asked. "You don't expect a woman to do the work of a deckhand, do you?"

Johnny cracked his sardonic smile once again. "I'll make it easy on you. I'm a fair man. I'll pay you a hand's wage."

"Out of what we already gave you, you mean?"

Johnny crossed his arms. "I'm a fair man. Foul too, but mostly fair."

*

The ship moved past a large cliff of white stone that descended into a pile of rocks, defying the grinding surf and remaining jagged and ugly. A wide cove opened up on the other side, filled with turquoise water and sands as pale as the rocks. The sea was calm inside the cove and sparkled with the morning sun. At the captain's barked orders, two of the sailors hurried to the bow of the ship and trimmed the foresails and jibs. The ship slowed and begin bobbing very gently.

"That's quite a sight," Rone said, squinting his eyes from beneath his wide-brimmed hat. "Pity nobody lives out here to enjoy it."

"Not much reason to be out here, anymore. Pretty views don't make up for a bad harbor and bad soil." Farthow was stripped down to his waist and was busy stuffing his clothes and other implements into a leather bag. "But it does have its uses to the Count. You may not be able to see it, but there's a path in that deep-set ravine of rocks carved out by an old creek." Farthow pointed to a dark scar in the mottled white cliffs. "You can follow that up and out and make your way to the west side of Masala. Keep it in mind if you ever need to slip back in unnoticed."

"So, you won't be going to the mainland with us then?" Charlotte asked.

"Not today. I may have to go in a bit if a particular piece of the master's business doesn't sort itself out. Till then I have other duties within the city. Shadows to hide in, eaves to drop, the usual business." Farthow slung his bag across his back, the strap running from his right shoulder to his left hip. He dropped his voice to sound just above the wind. "Before I go, keep a few things in mind. The captain knows too much. I recommend you part company when you find it convenient, perhaps Nantien. It would also be wise to keep using aliases." Farthow began putting his blades into a second tightly constructed leather bag, which had an oversized cork bottle cap on the end.

"I've known the wisdom in that since before we got here, but we'll keep traveling under other guises," Rone said.

"Make sure of it. No doubt there will be a price on your head and her body after today, and I imagine it will be quite large. Last piece of advice: beware of trickery. If it's an agent of mine or the count's, we'll bear a Masala green and maroon flag, but only trust it if there is a stripe of gold thread between the two. It's our hidden detail. Likewise, only trust messages bearing a seal with a gold, green, and maroon ribbon. That is the only way you will know it is truly from our camp. Other people may now suspect our assistance, so you must not overlook that detail."

"Thank you. You shall have me if you need me," Rone said, extending his hand.

"I'll keep you to that, Rone." The two shook hands. "I've got to get back. Thanks for the adventure of this evening and morning. A life that isn't dull is one to hold on to."

"Farewell, and thanks for everything," Charlotte said. "I will remember it, whatever my fate."

Farthow looked hard in her eyes for a moment before turning to face the turquoise cove and white cliffs.

"Almost forgot," Farthow said, turning back suddenly. He jogged up to the stair to the quarter deck. He pulled a small leather bag from his pocket and threw it to Johnny. He shouted, "The Count appreciates your burden and your discretion in all matters."

Johnny felt the weight of the bag. He shook his head. "You bunch are a heap of trouble. And cheap bastards, too."

"Remember what I told you!" With that, Farthow dove off the side of the ship and plunged into the water. Small fish leaped out of the waves as he splashed. He surfaced with his two packs floating behind him and began to swim to shore.

"Watch out!" Johnny yelled as a rope flew over the heads of Charlotte and Rone, snapping taut as one of the sails filled with air. Two sailors worked to slacken the sail, letting it fill more deeply with wind, and the boat began to rock before slowly moving away from the land. Charlotte and Rone watched Farthow reach the shore and disappear into the foliage as the ship picked up speed, heading northeast. "Once we get out into the proper channel wind, let's unfurl those mainsails and get moving!" Johnny yelled to two other sailors standing mid-deck.

"He sure was insistent about the gold thread," Charlotte said quietly to Rone.

"It's because he's sure to send word for us, otherwise he probably wouldn't have bothered," Rone said. "That's not what I wanted." He turned and walked toward the forecastle, stopping to lean on a rail and look to the north. "But we're alive and on our way. I'll gladly take on a debt for that."

"Thank you," Charlotte said. She stood beside him, watching him rather than the ocean. "You could have left me."

Rone looked at her and frowned. "I told you to have a little faith."

"I have more than a little now."

Rone smiled slightly. "Good. There's a long way left to go still. Hopefully less trouble, but if not, at least I know I've got a decent marksman at my side."

"I hired you to deal with the dirty work," Charlotte said, smiling. "The way I see it, I already ought to dock your pay."

Rone broadened his smile. "If I was just in it for the money, I'd have turned you over to Farthow."

"Why didn't you?"

Rone shrugged. "I'm weak to a pretty face, I guess."

Charlotte looked out to the sea, blushing slightly. "I won't complain about it."

End of Book I

ABOUT THE AUTHOR

David Van Dyke Stewart is an author, musician, YouTuber, and educator who currently lives in rural California with his wife and children.

He is the author of *Muramasa: Blood Drinker, Water of Awakening,* the *Needle Ash* series, and *The Crown of Sight,* as well as numerous novellas, essays, and short stories. He is also the primary performer in the music project *David V. Stewart's Zul.*

You can find his YouTube channel at http://www.youtube.com/rpmfidel where he creates content on music education, literary analysis, movie analysis, philosophy, and logic.

Sign up to his mailing list at http://dvspress.com/list for a free book and advance access to future projects. You can email any questions or concerns to stu@dvspress.com.

Be sure to check http://davidvstewart.com and http://dvspress.com for news and free samples of all his books.

Made in the USA
Coppell, TX
28 April 2021

54640128R00080